This book belongs to:

David Walliams

PRESENTS...

For Rockefeller,
with oodles of love,
Uncle David x

For Zoë,
with love – A.S.

First published in hardback by HarperCollins *Children's Books* in 2020
HarperCollins *Children's Books* is a division of HarperCollins*Publishers* Ltd.
Text © David Walliams 2020. Illustrations © Adam Stower 2020.
Cover lettering of author's name © Quentin Blake 2010
David Walliams and Adam Stower assert the moral right to be identified as the author and illustrator of the work respectively.
A CIP catalogue record for this book is available from the British Library.

1 London Bridge Street, London SE1 9GF.
1 3 5 7 9 10 8 6 4 2
Printed and bound in Italy.
978-0-00-830574-1

Visit our website at:
www.harpercollins.co.uk

LITTLE MONSTERS

ILLUSTRATED
BY THE AMAZING

*Adam
Stower*

HarperCollins *Children's Books*

Whenever there was a **full moon**, **Howler** howled so **high** . . .

"HOOHOOHOO!"

. . . that all the other werewolves howled with laughter.

"HA! HA! HA!"

Howler hated feeling like the **odd one out**. So Papa werewolf and Mama werewolf sent their son off to Monster School where he could learn how to be frightening.

MONSTER SCHOOL

TOWN

Woods

But Howler found the **school** frightening. He wasn't sure WHO to be more afraid of . . .

the **teachers** . . .

or the **pupils**.

Howler took a seat at the back of the classroom.
Suddenly, his teacher *whooshed* in on her broomstick,
SMASHING the skeleton to pieces as she did so.

CLA

"The first lesson of the day," announced
Miss Spell, "is how to pull a SCARY FACE.
Show me your scariest one!"

The vampire
flashed his fangs.

The ghost grinned a
ghoulish grin.

TTER!

The **skeleton** showed a sinister **smile**.

All eyes turned to Howler . . .

"You!" snarled Miss Spell,
pointing at her new pupil.

"Y-y-yes, miss!"

"Show me your
SCARIEST face!
NOW!"

The little werewolf did his best.

He **bulged out** his eyes,

waggled his ears

and **stuck out** his tongue.

Instead of looking **scary**, he looked like he was **blowing off**.
All the other little monsters HOOTED with laughter.

"HA! HA! HA!"

"You couldn't scare a FLY!"
mocked the teacher.

"The second lesson of the day is SPOOKING!"
announced Miss Spell in the school hall.

The witch ordered the mummy to
stand still with his back turned.

One by one,
the little monsters
did their best to
creep up on him.

The vampire
flew.

The ghost
floated.

The skeleton rattled.

Finally, it was Howler's turn.
The little werewolf was so nervous he tripped up over his tail.

TRIP!

He tumbled over and over again . . .

ROLL!

. . . landing by the skeleton's feet.

THUD!

"HA! HA! HA!
You couldn't scare a FLEA!"
snorted Spell.

Next, the teacher led
the little monsters
down steep stone steps.

"The final lesson of the day is
gruesome GROWLS," she said, her voice
echoing around the dark dungeon.

Oh no! thought the little werewolf
with the squeakiest voice.
My worst nightmare!

"HISS!"
went the vampire.

"WUHUHUH!"
went the ghost.

"SNARL!"
went the skeleton.

Trembling with fear, Howler howled **higher** than ever.

"WOOOHOOO!"

"HA!"

HA!

HA!"

"HOWLER!" bawled Miss Spell. "You couldn't scare a NIT! You're a disgrace to Monster School! To the headmaster's office! AT ONCE!"

"Howler, you will never, EVER be a monster!" boomed Mr Ogre.

"P-p-please, s-s-sir . . ."

"YOU ARE EXPELLED FROM MONSTER SCHOOL!"

A tear welled in Howler's eye.

Skulking back home to the forest, the werewolf spotted another group of little monsters going door to door and saying,

"TRICK OR TREAT?"

These monsters were different. As he drew closer,
Howler saw that they were little humans
dressed up as MONSTERS.

It was HALLOWEEN!

"WOW! Cool werewolf costume!" said an alien on spotting him.

"Are you on your own?" asked a spider.

Howler nodded sheepishly.
None of the kids realised Howler
was a **real-life** werewolf.

"Come and join us!" said a shark.

"Thanks!" exclaimed Howler, smiling for the first time in ages.

"You look so SCARY! You can go at the front!" said the alien.

Howler wasn't so sure. He gulped before he knocked on the first door, sure he couldn't even scare a nit.

Knock!
Knock!
Knock!

But before the werewolf could even say "TRICK OR TREAT?" the man at the door screamed. "ARGH!"

He threw a hail of sweets at the little monsters.

The kids caught them and were over the moon. They had never had so many treats.

With Howler leading the pack, the same thing happened at house after house.

"YIKES!"

Soon more and more little monsters from all over town joined in the FUN.

As no one dared to say "TRICK" to the little werewolf, there were treats for everyone!

Now it was **late** and they'd knocked on all the doors.
The little monsters were stuffed full of sweets
and ready to head home to bed. But there was still
one more person Howler was determined to scare.

Can you **guess** WHO?

"Just ONE more!
Follow me!" he said.

Soon they had reached MONSTER SCHOOL.

"When I hold up my paw,
I want you ALL to do your LOUDEST howl!"
announced Howler.

All the kids grinned from ear to ear.
This was going to be FUN!

"*SHUSH!*" hissed Howler as they crept into the classroom where Miss Spell was busy marking homework.

Howler raised his paw, and he led them all in the LOUDEST howl.

"WOOHOOHOOHOOHOOHOO!"

"ARGH!" screamed the teacher, shooting out of her chair.

WHOOSH!

She bounced off the ceiling . . .

BOING!

. . . she bounced off the walls . . .

BOING!

BOING!

. . . she bounced off the floor . . .

BOING!

. . . before bouncing **right into** the **headmaster**, who had appeared at the door.

W_aLL_OP!

"WHAT IS THE MEANING OF THIS?"
thundered Mr Ogre as the little monsters helped him up.

"It looks like I CAN scare, after all, sir!" replied Howler.

The headmaster looked down at the crumpled witch by his feet.
Miss Spell was out cold!

"Howler! I was wrong.
You ARE scary!
May I welcome you back to
Monster School?"

The little werewolf looked round at the kids in costumes . . .

"No thanks! I am going to stick with my new friends."

All the little monsters broke out into a howl of happiness.

"WooHOO!"

What about Papa werewolf and Mama werewolf?
They couldn't have been happier that their son
was happy just being himself.

Howler **did** go to school with his **new friends**.

So when YOU are at school have a look around your classroom.

Sitting at the back there **might** just be a little monster.

It's cool to be the ODD one out.

"ARGH!"

"WOOHOOHOOHOOHOOHOO!"

This book belongs to

_____

_____

For
Wilbur
Jones

First published 2020 by Macmillan Children's Books
an imprint of Pan Macmillan
The Smithson, 6 Briset Street, London EC1M 5NR
Associated companies throughout the world
www.panmacmillan.com

ISBN: 978-1-5290-2137-0

Text and illustrations copyright © Jill Murphy 2020
Moral rights asserted

1 3 5 7 9 8 6 4 2

A CIP catalogue record is available for this book from the British Library.

Printed in China

Just One of Those Days

Jill Murphy

MACMILLAN CHILDREN'S BOOKS

It had been a long night . . .

. . . so Mr and Mrs Bear woke up late.

They left Baby Bear dreaming
of dinosaurs while they got ready
for work.

Then they woke Baby Bear and got him ready for Nursery, which took even longer than usual.

Outside, it was raining. Mr Bear got the bus and Mrs Bear took Baby Bear to Nursery on her way to work.

Nursery had already started by the time
they got there.

In the cloakroom, Baby Bear wouldn't
take his coat off.

"I want to go home," he said, in a very
small voice.

Mrs Bear took Baby Bear to join the class.
His teacher was reading them a story.

"*There* you are!" she said. "In you come."

After the story, Baby Bear saw that
Someone Else was playing with his
best dinosaur.
"MINE!" he yelled.
"No, no," said his teacher. "Come and play
with Diplodocus instead. He's just as nice."
Baby Bear tried hard to like Diplodocus,
but his mouth didn't open and he didn't
have purple blotches – so it was difficult.

At work, Mrs Bear sat on her glasses and Mr Bear spilt coffee all over an important pile of papers.

At Nursery, when it was lunchtime, Someone Else got the red cup. The water didn't taste as nice in the green one.

At work, Mr Bear didn't have time for lunch. He was too busy reprinting the messed-up papers – and Mrs Bear fell asleep half-way through her blueberry muffin.

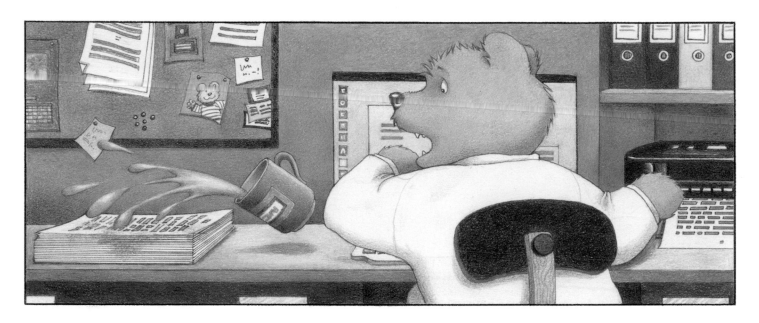

At Nursery, after lunch they did painting, which was nice, but Someone Else had used all the purple paint.

Then they did cooking, which got a bit messy.

Then they did dancing, which got a bit tricky.
"I want you all to dance like trees in the wind," said their teacher.

By the end of the day, Baby Bear could
hardly keep his eyes open. He was so
glad to see his Mum waiting for him.
It was still raining as they trudged
home together.
"Daddy's bringing in a pizza," said Mrs Bear,
"so we don't have to cook."
When they got home, Mrs Bear and
Baby Bear got into their comfy pyjamas.

"Daddy's home!" yelled Baby Bear.
Mr Bear came in, with a big pizza box
and a carrier bag.
"Look in the bag," he said. "It's something
for you."

Baby Bear dived into the bag and brought out
– T. Rex!
"He's exactly the same as the one you always
play with at Nursery," said Mr Bear proudly.
"I saw him in a shop window and thought you
might like to have one of your very own."

Baby Bear tested the jaw to make sure
it moved. Then he hugged Mr Bear
very tightly.
Then he took off the labels.

Then he and T. Rex roared, and chased
Mum and Dad into the kitchen.
"Better get this pizza on to plates,"
said Mrs Bear, "before *someone* goes
into orbit!"

"How was work?" asked Mr Bear, as they made their way to the sofa with their pizza.

"Not brilliant," said Mrs Bear. "How about you?"

"Not brilliant," said Mr Bear. "I think it was just one of those days."

"Never mind," said Mrs Bear. "We can have a better one tomorrow – why don't we all go to bed early?"

"Good idea," said Mr Bear. "I'll do the bedtime story . . ."

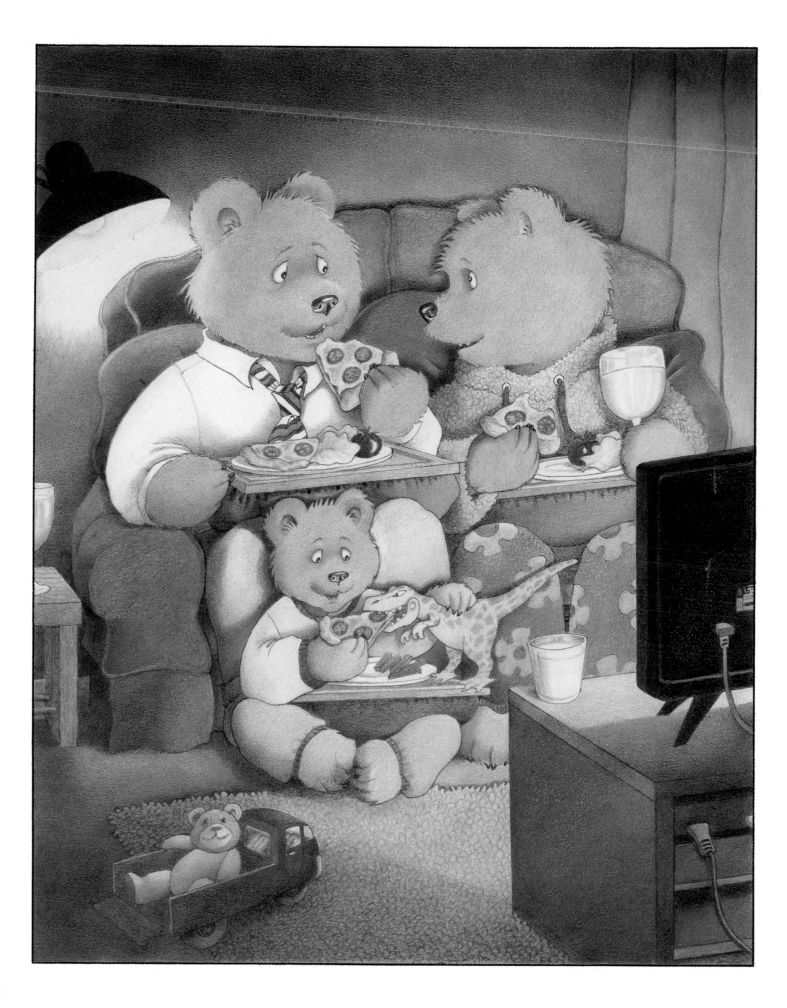

. . . and he did.

emma brennan

making **vintage** bags

20 original sewing patterns for vintage **bags** and **purses**

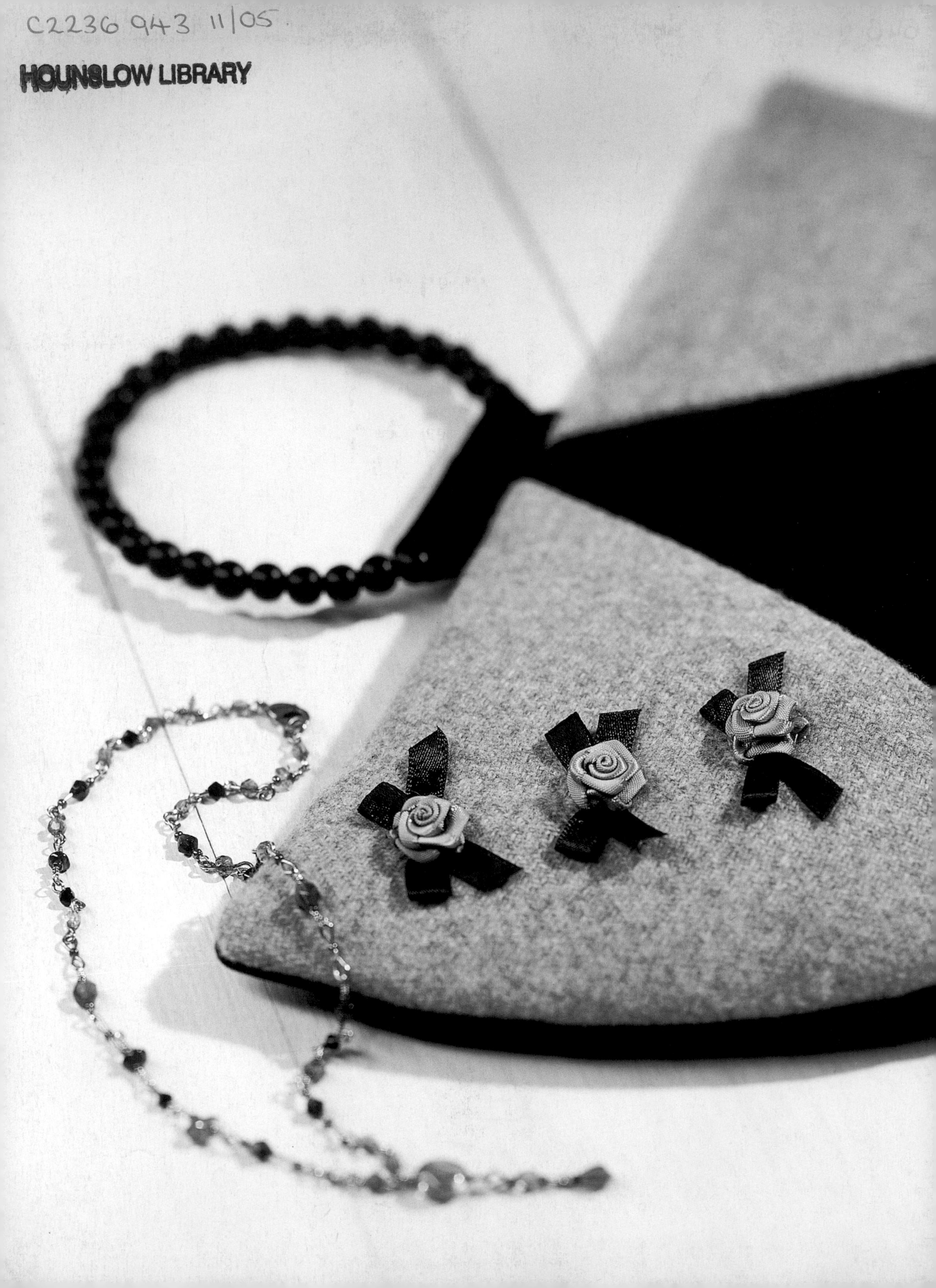

making vintage bags

20 original sewing patterns for vintage **bags** and **purses**

emma brennan

GUILD OF MASTER CRAFTSMAN PUBLICATIONS

First published 2005 by

Guild of Master Craftsman Publications Ltd

166 High Street, Lewes

East Sussex, BN7 1XU

Text and bag design © Emma Brennan 2005

© in the work Guild of Master Craftsman Publications Ltd

ISBN 1 86108 411 0

British Cataloguing in Publication Data

A catalogue record of this book is available from the British Library.

Managing Editor	Gerrie Purcell
Production Manager	Hilary MacCallum
Photography	Gill Orsman, Anthony Bailey
Editor	Clare Miller
Art Editor	Gilda Pacitti

Colour reproduction by Altaimage Ltd.
Printed and bound by Hing Yip Printing Co. Ltd.

This book is dedicated to Sarah and Dad – constant inspiration, constantly missed.

Note:

Although care has been taken to ensure that metric measurements are true and accurate, they are only conversions from imperial; they have been rounded up or down to the nearest cm, or to the nearest convenient equivalent in cases where the imperial measurements themselves are only approximate. When following the projects, use either imperial or metric measurements; do not mix units.

foreword

Beautiful bags have been the obsession of many a fashion conscious lady for decades. Before the currently huge selection of mass-produced bags became available through high street shops, women would make their own. Sometimes leftover fabric scraps would be used to make a cherished one-off creation, perhaps to tie in with or add a finishing flourish to an outfit.

Handbags have come full circle. At present the trend is for vintage-style bags and bags which are individual or handmade, but with price tags for this type of bag being beyond most people's budgets, it's a useful and rewarding skill to be able to make your own.

A handbag can make a statement as well as being a practical means of carrying your essential possessions around. This book gives you patterns and ideas for making your own special bag, influenced by vintage styles but perfect for modern living.

This book offers a selection of my own unique vintage-inspired designs, made using workable patterns and easily accessible modern materials. Each style is shown in a particular fabric, but there are also tips on ways to vary each bag and ideas for making your own bag unique.

I hope that you enjoy creating the bags in the book and that it gives you the confidence to go on and create your own unique pieces using different combinations of fabrics, shapes, handles and embellishments.

Emma Brennan

contents

1920s

1930s

1940s

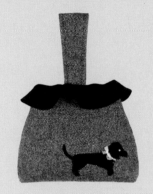

martha

page 86

veronica

page 92

grace

page 98

patricia

page 102

rose

page 106

1950s

audrey

page 112

vivien

page 116

shirley

page 120

peggy

page 124

gloria

page 130

materials and techniques

This section explains what you need to make a bag and covers all of the main techniques used throughout the book to create the 20 beautiful bag projects that follow.

Using the pattern templates, choosing fabrics, using base materials, lining bags, making handles and fixing fastenings are all covered in step-by-step instructions that follow through the assembly of sample bags.

In the next section of the book, the projects themselves have detailed step-by-step instructions, but are illustrated with pictures only where a technique differs from the standard method outlined here. It is essential therefore that you read and understand the methods outlined with pictures in this introductory section before you go on to attempt any of the individual projects.

Basic sewing techniques are not covered in the book. It is assumed that the reader will have knowledge of rudimentary sewing skills. It is not necessary to be an expert – I have taught some of the projects in the book to students with no knowledge of bag-making, but with good basic sewing skills and all have completed unique and very usable bags to be proud of.

bag-making basics

To make the bags in this book you will need the following equipment and materials:

✲ A paper pattern template copied from the book

✲ Suitable fabric for the bag

✲ Backing fabric to stiffen or bulk up the main fabric

✲ Handle

✲ Fastener

✲ Fabric to line the bag

✲ Embellishment materials or trims

✲ Sewing machine (with zipper foot option)

✲ A flat iron

✲ Basic sewing kit consisting of dressmaking scissors, pins, needles and tape measure

useful additional equipment

✲ Rotating hole punch (for leather/fabric)

✲ Appliqué or small sharp scissors

how to use the patterns in the book

Patterns for all the bags are printed at the back of the book, from page 134 onwards. They are reproduced at a reduced size and are designed to be enlarged using a photocopier. When enlarging, ensure that the black arrow on each page is always placed in the top left corner of the photocopier and that the dotted rule is aligned with the top edge of the glass. The easiest way is to take the book to a photocopy shop and get the pattern sheets enlarged onto A3 size paper following these instructions. The pattern pieces will then be the correct size to cut out and use straight away.

Where the same pattern pieces are used for two different styles of bag, the templates have clear directions for both on them. Some of the larger pattern pieces, which did not fit onto an A4 sheet when reduced, have been drawn 'on the fold' (see below) which means that the piece needs to be cut on the fold of the fabric or redrawn on the fold of a larger piece of paper before use.

to cut out your bag

First enlarge the relevant pattern templates and cut them out. Lay the pattern pieces onto the fabric following the directions given within the project. You should pin the pattern pieces onto the fabric and cut around them with dressmaking scissors.

If a pattern template has **fold line** written along an edge, this means that you must place this edge of the pattern along a fold in the fabric when you are cutting out the bag. In effect, the template is 'half' of the piece – by cutting on the fold you will cut out the other half at the same time. The instructions for each project will remind you when a piece needs to be cut on the fold. If you prefer, you can redraw the template with the 'on fold' edge along the folded edge of a larger piece of paper to make the pattern piece full size before you start cutting the fabric.

remember to enlarge all pattern pieces by 165%

sewing tip

Note that the relevant **seam allowances** have already been added to the patterns in this book.

and techniques

11

materials

basic stitches

The majority of the sewing for the projects in this book is completed with a sewing machine. Unless otherwise stated, a standard sewing machine foot is used and a regular length straight stitch. At the beginning and end of each seam, you must make a few back-stitches to secure the seam. A zigzag stitch (**A**) is also used for appliqué and neatening the edges on trims. A zipper foot is used for inserting zippers and for close stitching around handles.

There are just a few hand-stitches throughout the book, which will be referred to in several of the projects.

basting

Basting, also known as 'tacking', is referred to in all of the projects. Basting is temporary stitching which is not essential to the structure of the bag, but merely holds things in place until you stitch them together properly. Basting can either be done by hand, or on a sewing machine. If basting by hand (**B**), simply use a straight running stitch. If basting by machine, use a very long length straight stitch.

gathering

Another stitch which is used on the centre of bows, and on fabric flowers or leaves, is the gathering stitch. This is just a basic running stitch which is then pulled up to form gathers. It is advisable to use a double thickness of thread for this stitch.

tailor's tacks

In some cases it is possible to transfer the special marker points from the paper pattern onto the cut fabric or interfacing pieces using a soft pencil. Where this is not appropriate, especially where you wish to transfer markers to a double thickness of fabric, you should use tailors tacks. To make these, thread a needle with a long double thickness of thread. Use a colour which will show up well against your fabric. Make a stitch through both layers of fabric at the marker point (**C**). Cut the thread leaving two tails around 3in (8cm) in length. Take off the pattern piece. Carefully separate the two layers of fabric and snip the threads in between (**D**). This will leave a thread marker at the same point on both pieces of fabric.

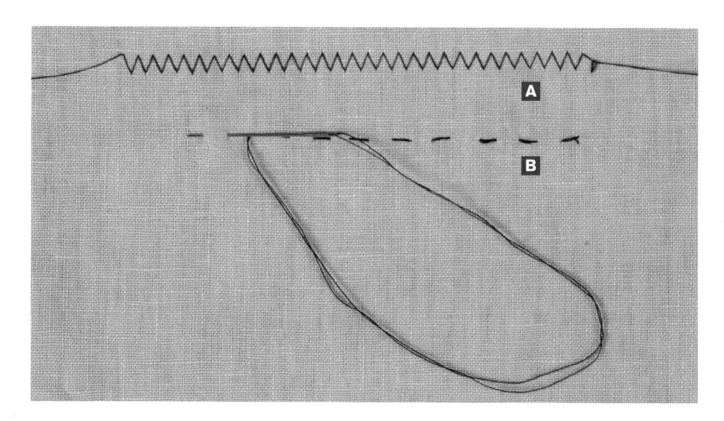

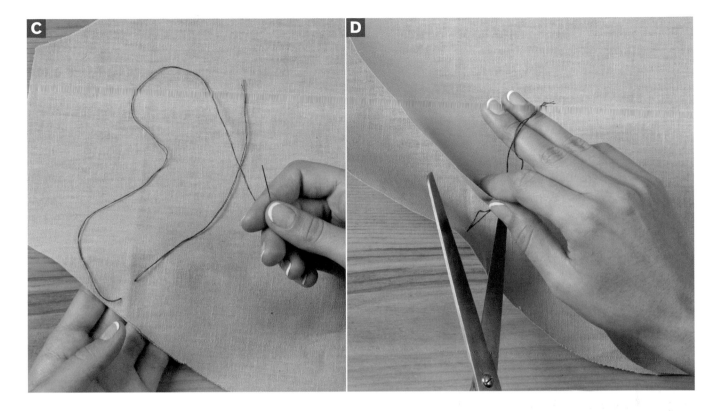

slip-stitch

Most of the projects have a gap in the lining through which the bag is turned right side out. You will be instructed to 'slip-stitch' the opening closed (**E**). This means that you should hand-stitch the opening neatly to avoid a bulky seam.

whipstitch

In projects that have a zipper set into the top or back, you will be required to whipstitch the open ends of the zipper tape together. Whipstitching is the way in which two pieces that are laying side by side are joined together using a stitch that goes in on one piece and comes out on the other. It is sometimes referred to as an 'oversewing' stitch and can be used for protecting edges. In the case of a zipper you should whipstitch about five or six times in the same spot to hold the two sides of the zipper together flat (**F**).

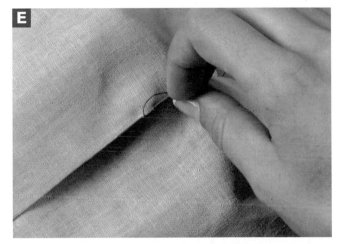

fabrics

In this book, I have given the approximate quantity or yardage of fabric, lining and interfacing needed to make each project. As most people still buy fabric by the yard or metre I have given the length of fabric you would need to buy off the roll first. The minimum width of the fabric you would need for that length is also given. If you are buying off the roll, the width of fabric is usually given on the price ticket or roll centre in inches or centimetres. Adjust the lengths accordingly if you are buying narrower width fabric. Dimensions and yardage are given in imperial measurements (inches) first and then in metric (centimetres or millimetres) in brackets afterwards. For materials needed, the conversion from inches to centimetres is rounded up to the nearest centimetre and is not intended to be a precise conversion.

Many of the bags are suitable projects for using up smaller remnant pieces. Just cut out the pattern template pieces and try laying them on the fabric. You'll be surprised what you can get out of a small piece of material.

You can make bags out of virtually any fabric from delicate silk to hard-wearing cotton twill. If you want to make a vintage-style bag, you could use original vintage fabric. Bags take very little fabric to make so you could pick up a small piece of vintage textile for a reasonable price. However, some vintage fabric may actually be too delicate to make a functional bag with. You can use some original vintage trims if you want to include a genuine piece of history. This will be discussed later under **Embellishments** (see page 33).

For a modern vintage bag, you are probably better off buying some of the wonderful vintage-style fabrics on the market instead. Some modern materials have a more 'vintage' look than others. Fabrics like velvet, corduroy, tweed/wool and brocade for example, have been used in fashion for centuries. Furnishing fabrics are also a good choice for bags as they are often more solid and durable. Luckily, the current trend for furnishing fabrics is also quite retrospective, which means that there are some wonderful vintage and 'retro' prints and stripes around – ideal for bag-making.

Colour is a very important factor too. Choosing fabrics in 'muted' or faded colours can really add to the vintage look. Fabric dyes in the last century tended to be more subtle, and home fashion catalogues of the first half of the 1900s advertised must-have accessories in colours like rust tan, flying blue, coffee, rosewine and lido beige. Even the names of the colours conjure up nostalgic images.

I have used a variety of fabrics, from those that are more traditional, like wool and corduroy, for day bags, to more lavish textiles, like silk brocade and velvet for evening bags and fabrics with a vintage appearance like ticking stripe and faded florals. You can make any of the patterns up in different fabrics if you prefer, but the fabrics I've chosen are suited to the particular style and feel of each bag. There are tips for using a particular fabric alongside the individual projects.

Generally, when choosing a fabric for your project, firstly you must decide on the use for the bag (day or evening, beach bag or shopper etc) and then you must decide if you want the bag to have a 'soft' feel or if you want it to be more stiff and rigid. Although some fabrics are not very stiff or durable on their own, any fabric can be bulked up by using a 'base' material. Therefore, choosing a suitable base material for your bag is as important as finding the main fabric.

structure and suitable base materials

One thing to bear in mind is that a 'handmade' bag will never have the structure of a purchased modern bag. Most mass-produced bags are made in factories, using heavily bonded and stiffened materials, and specialist sewing equipment. That lack of 'hardness' which is characteristic of a handmade bag is part of its appeal, giving it a 'home grown' feel. Vintage home sewing patterns for bags in the 1930s and 40s recommend the use of stiffening materials such as crinoline, muslin and tarlatan. Modern versions, known widely as 'interfacing' or 'interlining', are available in a wide variety of weights and density, most of them being more easy to handle and work with than their vintage counterparts. Interfacings are used to give a good foundation and can also prevent stretching, especially around the top of the bag. There are many options for base materials for making a handmade bag today. The following are used for the projects in the book.

iron-on or fusible interfacing

These are usually only suitable for fabrics that can be ironed at fairly high temperatures. Makes like Vilene, non-woven synthetic fibres are readily available in a variety of weights and are easy to use. They are used in this book for several of the projects.

sew-in craft weight (or pelmet) interfacing

A durable material which can have a soft or hard feel. This adds weight and structure and can be used for most fabrics as it doesn't have to be ironed on. Used in this book for many of the projects where a more defined shape is required.

wadding (also known as 'batting')

A soft but substantial material which adds 'bulk' and padding without stiffness. Wadding is usually sewn in, although there are now some fusible brands on the market. Used in this book between layers for quilting and on some of the softer bags.

Others not used in the book include **buckram** or **canvas** materials – these are more expensive to use as interfacing fabrics but they are long-lasting, durable and give a tailored look.

plastic canvas

This is plastic mesh which is used for cross-stitch. It is used in the book for cutting out a 'base' rectangle to insert in the bottom of a bag. This gives shape and a firm base to the project. Some patterns advocate the use of thick cardboard. Plastic canvas however is a more durable material.

fusible web

Although not a 'base' material, fusible web is invaluable for fusing two layers of textile together. It usually comes with a paper backing which can be drawn onto and ironed over to fuse it to the fabric. It is used in this book for fusing appliqué to the front of bags before stitching and to make professional-looking fabric handles. Well known makes include Bondaweb in the UK and HeatnBond in the US.

piece preparation

Interfacing pieces for bags should be stitched or fused to the relevant fabric pieces before assembling the bag. Remember to only use fusible (iron-on) interfacings on bag pieces which are made of suitable fabrics. Do not use fusible interfacings on fake leather/suede. These synthetic fabrics often cannot be ironed and even if you do manage to successfully fuse the interfacing to the fabric, it invariably comes 'unstuck' over time and can give a 'bubbly' appearance. Ironing interfacing onto velvet will also crush the pile – this is why I have used very short pile cotton velveteen for the projects in this book, which can be successfully used with fusible interfacing.

iron-on interfacing

Before you start assembling your bag, attach interfacing to all of the relevant pieces. If you are using a fabric which is compatible with fusible interfacing, you can simply iron the fusible interfacing pieces onto the reverse side of the fabric. It is often necessary to use a little steam or a damp cloth to help release the bonding unit in the interfacing. Ensure that the interfacing is completely stuck down all over, particularly around the edges. For best results, always follow the manufacturer's instructions for the brand of interfacing you are using.

wadding

Attach cut-out fabric pieces to wadding in the same way as you would sew-in interfacing. However, you may find it easier in the case of wadding to baste from the fabric side. This will prevent the machine foot from becoming entangled in the wadding. Wadding can also warp out of shape slightly after being cut. After you have basted the wadding to the fabric you may need to trim any excess wadding from around the edge of the pieces before assembling the bag.

using sew-in interfacing

If your fabric is not compatible with iron-on interfacing, you must baste-stitch the relevant bag pieces to the interfacing pieces before you start assembling the bag.

Step 1

First lay the interfacing pieces on the reverse side of the corresponding fabric pieces. Pin from the right side, using pins at an angle so that they can be left in while machine-basting (**A**). Leaving the pins in will avoid the need to hand-baste, but if you feel more comfortable hand-basting, you can do so. Smooth out any wrinkles as you pin.

Step 2

Using a long stitch length, machine-baste fabric and interfacing together around the entire outside edge of each piece. Use a seam allowance of about ¼in (6mm) from the outside edge. If you stitch from the interfacing side, this will help to avoid the fabric puckering or moving as you stitch.

assembling a bag after interfacing

Once both the front and back sections of the bag have been interfaced, you can begin to assemble the bag. Some of the bags have a more three-dimensional shape rather than being completely flat. For these designs, you will have to fold the lower corners of the bag to form a gusset.

Step 1
Pin the two interfaced front/back sections **right sides together**. Stitch round sides and lower edges, leaving a ½in (13mm) seam allowance (**A**).

Step 2
If the bag has a gusset, fold the lower corners of the bag, matching seams, and pin and baste in place (**B**).

Step 3
Stitch straight across lower corners to form gusset (**C**). Repeat this on the opposite corner.

Step 4
Turn bag right sides out and press (**D**).

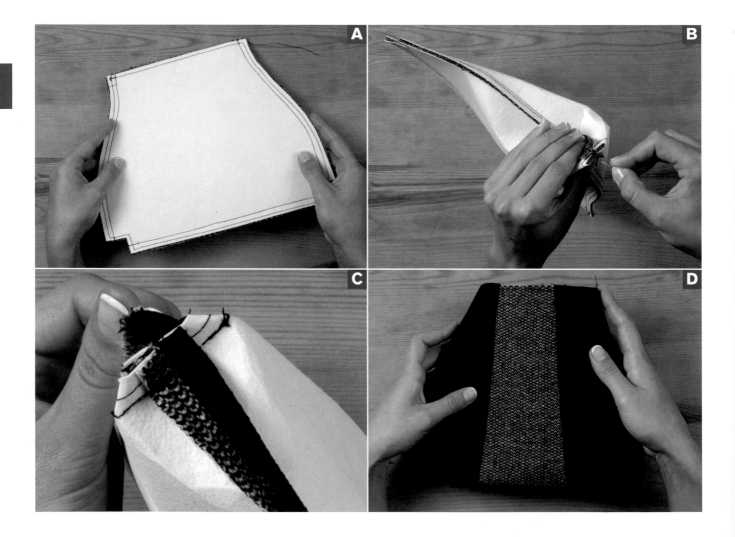

handles

Once the bag has been turned right side out, you must attach the handle at this point, before lining the bag. The handle has to be sandwiched between the bag and the lining.

When making a handmade bag, you can either use commercially produced bag handles or you can be inventive and make your own. Most of the projects in this book use handmade handles. Ready-made handles are often quite expensive, although they can give a professional finish to a bag. Handmade handles however are always a bit more special, and probably more in keeping with a hand-crafted vintage-style bag.

In general, what you need to consider when choosing a handle is whether you want to carry the bag in your hand, on your shoulder, across your body or tucked under your arm. The length and size of the handles you use will be determined by the style of bag and how you wish to carry it.

some handle options

* purchased 'ring' handles in bamboo, plastic or metal
* purchased long straight handles in wood or plastic
* purchased rope or braid
* handmade flat fabric handles, made from matching or contrasting fabric, sometimes trimmed with ribbon
* beaded handles (purchased or handmade) made using heavy gauge wire with wooden beads
* wooden ring or doweling, painted with acrylic paints to match your fabric and sealed with varnish
* plastic, metal or wooden bangles

and techniques

19

materials

making **vintage** bags

self-fabric handles

These are a really good option for many bags, especially if you find it difficult to acquire a handle that matches your chosen bag fabric. Many bag patterns make fabric handles by folding a piece of fabric in half lengthways, stitching a seam down the long side and then turning it through to form a long tube which is then pressed flat. This will suffice in many cases, particularly with shorter 'wrist' length straps, but it can be difficult to physically 'turn' a longer tube. This is further complicated if you are using a stiff fabric like tapestry or other furnishing fabrics.

I prefer to make handles that do not require turning. The following method can be applied to all kinds of fabric, and is used for many of the projects in this book.

Step 1
First cut out the fabric strip for each handle according to the measurements given in the pattern. Then cut out a strip of fusible web the same size as the fabric handle. Iron the fusible web to the handle, paper side up, according to the manufacturer's guidelines.

Step 2
Next, fold in the long edges of the fabric handle strip to the centre on each side, so that they meet in the middle and press with a damp cloth to fuse (**A**).

Step 3
From here, you can complete the handle in two ways.

Ribbon method
Firstly you can pin a strip of ribbon down the centre of the turned-in handle covering the join, and top-stitch it down each side (**B**). The ribbon should be slightly narrower than the finished width of the turned-in fabric handle. You can fix the handle, ribbon side out if you are using a velvet or decorative ribbon (**C**). If you are using grosgrain or backing ribbon then fix the handles ribbon side under. With this method, the handle will end up being half the width of the original fabric strip.

Alternative method

With the second method, when you have turned both long edges in and fused them in place, you can then fold the handle in half lengthways again, pin and machine stitch it together down the unfolded edge (**D**).

This method makes a narrower handle and is not as suitable for bulky fabrics. With this method, the handle will end up being a quarter of the width of the original fabric strip (**E**).

attaching the handle to the bag

Handles must be attached to the bag before the bag is lined, and in the case of the bags with back zipper openings where the handle is set into the top seam, before the front and back are joined.

For a top-opening bag, once the front and back are stitched together and turned right sides out, the handle must be attached, with right side of handle flat against the right side of the bag, with the handle facing downwards (**A**).

The handle will then be sandwiched between the lining/facing and the bag, the ends of the handle will not be seen, and the handle will face upwards when the bag is finally lined and turned.

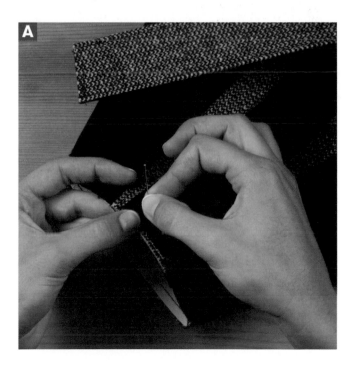

beaded ring handles

Several of the bags in this book have beaded ring handles. These can be made using the following materials and steps.

To make a beaded ring handle, you will require beads with large centre holes and wire in a heavy weight (gauge). Craft wire can be sized either by gauge or in millimetres. The wire used to make the handles in this book is 16 gauge, or 1.2mm.

To make one handle, around 4in (10cm) in diameter, you will need approximately 14in (36cm) of wire and 26 wooden beads (size 8 to 10mm or larger, with large central holes). If you use longer or larger beads, you must adjust the quantity accordingly.

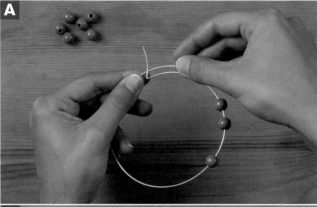

Step 1
The wire usually comes in a rounded loop, so you will not have to shape it. Cut a loop of wire the size of the handle you require, plus 2–3in (6–8cm). At one end of the loop, using pliers, turn up about 1in (25mm) (**A**).

Step 2
Thread on the beads until you have a handle the size you require, and then turn a bend in the wire directly after the last bead (**B**).

Step 3
Cut ends back to around 1in (25mm) each end, then twist together using pliers (**C**). The ring handle is attached to the bag front or back by means of a 'handle carrier'. This is a short, wider strip of fabric with long edges folded in to centre and fused using the same method as for the self-fabric handle. The finished strip is then folded around the handle and stitched to the bag before assembly. The join in the wire will not be seen as it will be inside the handle carrier.

fasteners

All bags need a fastener, and although you can add a vintage touch with the right choice of fastener, it still needs to be practical for modern living. When the pace of life was slower, fasteners on bags could be more decorative – current lifestyles mean that modern bags need to provide easy access. If you are going to use a bag daily, a practical closure is essential. For evening bags a more dressy touch can be added.

There are of course many other fasteners that you could use on a handmade bag. Some suggestions for alternative fasteners include ribbon ties – very pretty but not suitable for bags where you need to get in and out frequently, frog fasteners (**A**), which can be very decorative but are often not very easy to open in a hurry, or buttons. If using a button, for ease of opening use a large 'loop' with it rather than a button-hole. Ribbons and button loops need to be stitched between the bag and the lining (as for handles) during construction. Frog fasteners can be stitched on when the bag has been completed.

velcro

Velcro is a very modern invention and therefore not very vintage! However, if you cannot find magnetic snaps it can be used as an alternative. Although it can now be purchased in some different colours, limited ranges mean that it is often not possible to match it perfectly to your fabric. Where possible use an exact match, but failing this, black, white or neutral colours are best. It should generally only be used where it will not be seen from the outside.

Velcro has two parts – one part has tiny hooks on it and the other half has loops. The two halves 'stick' together and can be pulled apart with ease. Velcro is suitable for use with touch-and-close style bags, where each half of the fastener is fixed onto the lining or facing on the inside of the bag opposite to one another (as with the magnetic snaps). Velcro is fairly easy to apply. Transfer the snap markers on the pattern pieces to the right side of the relevant fabric facing or lining piece. Place the Velcro centrally over the markers, pin and stitch around the outside of each piece, using a short stitch length.

Alternatively, you could use large press stud fasteners as a substitute and just apply them at the magnetic snap marker positions. The advantage of these is that they can be stitched onto the bag after assembly.

magnetic snaps

Purchased magnetic snaps are the first choice of fastener for modern handbags, providing easy but secure closure, simple to apply and invisible from the outside of the bag. Available in a range of sizes and metal colour finishes they are ideal for use with flaps or 'touch-and-close' style bags.

A magnetic snap has four components (shown, right). One half of the snap is magnetic, the other metal half clicks into the centre of the magnet to snap shut. There are also two backing discs with holes in the centre that sit on the other side of the fabric. The 'prongs' on the back of the snaps are pushed through holes in the fabric then through these backing discs. The prongs are then bent back in an outward direction to secure

the fastener. In order to stabilize the fabric and give the snap a secure base, it is advisable to insert a small piece of craft interfacing between the back of the fabric and the backing disc.

Step 1
Transfer the snap position marks on the paper pattern template onto the relevant facing, lining or interfaced fabric pieces (where possible onto the interfacing or reverse side) using either a soft pencil or tailors tacks.

Step 2
Make two small holes through both thicknesses (fabric, and interfacing where relevant) using a leather hole punch if you have one, at the marker positions (they will be about ¼in (6mm) apart).

Step 3
Push the prongs of the 'non-magnetic' half of the clasp through the holes from the right side of the fabric, so that the snap part sits on the fabric side. This will be on the right side of the under part of the flap if you are making a bag with a flap, or on the right side of the inside facing if you are making a touch-and-close bag.

Step 4
Make two small holes in the centre of the snap stabilizer squares (1½in (38mm) square of craft interfacing), about ¼in (6mm) apart. Push the prongs of the snap through the holes in the snap stabilizer also (**A**). Put the backing disc of the snap over the prongs and bend the prongs outwards using pliers (**B**), so that this half of the snap is secure. Fix the second half in the same way.

lining

The lining of a bag is often an afterthought. However, you can really go to town with the choice of lining fabric if you are making your own bag. A fancy lining is a way to add a personal touch to a bag – a jaunty striped silk for example, provides an unexpected element when you open a plain wool bag. Bags can be lined with anything from printed polka dot, striped or plain cottons, to sumptuous silk jacquards. As you need so little fabric to line a bag, it's really worth using something a bit special.

Some of the projects in this book use quilted lining. This is usually acetate or satin which has been quilt stitched onto wadding. This gives extra padding to a bag without the need to use extra wadding, and in some cases means that you will only need to apply a light interfacing to the main bag pieces.

The intended use for the bag will often determine the type of lining to use. For example, a delicate silk lining would be more suited to an evening bag which will not be used frequently, whereas an everyday bag would be more durable if lined with a hard-wearing but pretty cotton fabric. The project bags in this book are lined with a variety of different fabrics. You can choose your own type of lining to suit your own purpose for the bag.

lining a bag

In this book, I line bags in different ways, but most using the same basic 'pull-through' method. In my own bags which open at the top, I like to use a 'facing' (made out of the same fabric as the main bag) so that you do not see the lining at the top of the bag. However, if you are using a particularly expensive or pretty lining that you want to be seen, then you can line right to the top of the bag and there will be no need for a facing. Many of the bags in the book are lined right to the top for ease of making.

before you line the bag

There are a few things to do before you can line your bag. Firstly, if you are adding a sew-in label, this should be machine stitched flat onto one side of the lining before assembly. You should also cut your plastic canvas rectangle for the base of the bag, ready to insert through the gap in the bottom of the lining when the bag is made. The other most important point is that if you are using a magnetic snap fastener, it is essential to attach it to the lining or facing before you line the bag (see below).

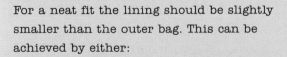

sewing tip

For a neat fit the lining should be slightly smaller than the outer bag. This can be achieved by either:

* stitching with a slightly greater seam allowance when stitching pieces together around side and lower edges, ie $^3/_4$in (18mm) instead of $^1/_2$in (13mm) all round.

* if lining to the top of the bag, cut about $^1/_2$in (13mm) off the upper edge of both lining pieces before assembling.

how to line a top-opening bag (with / without a facing)

Step 1
Take the two facing pieces and the two lining pieces. Pin lower edge of one facing to upper edge of one lining, right sides together. Sew them together using a regular stitch length then press seam towards lining.

Step 2
If you are sewing in a label or using a magnetic snap, these will need to be attached next, before you continue with the lining.

Step 3
Pin and stitch lining pieces right sides together at sides and lower edges, leaving an opening of around 4½in (12cm) in the centre of the lower edge. You will be 'turning' the bag through this opening. Ensure that the lining is slightly smaller than the finished bag so that it sits correctly and doesn't pucker up in the bag (**A**). Refer to the **Sewing Tip** on page 25.

Step 4
Stitch corner gussets if appropriate (following same method as main bag pieces).

Step 5
Insert bag into lining, and with right sides together, pin the facing/lining to the bag (over flap or handles if you have them) with upper edges even (**B**). Stitch around upper edge of bag with a ⅝in (15mm) seam allowance, through all thicknesses using a medium to long stitch length.

Note that depending on which kind of fabric you are using, there will be quite a lot of thicknesses to sew through (main fabric, interfacing, lining/facing, flap, handle), so stitch very slowly and carefully. Trim the seam back a little to eliminate bulk, and clip the seam allowance every inch (2.5cm) or so, especially near the side seams of the bag.

Step 6

Now you must 'turn' the bag right side out by pulling it through the opening in the bottom of the lining. At this point, once the bag is turned, you can gain access to the inside of the bag via the opening, so before closing the opening in the lining, insert your fingers through the opening to push any corners outward and shape any curves. When you are happy with the shape, give the bag a light press then insert plastic canvas in base through the opening in the lining (if appropriate). Slip-stitch the opening closed. Turn the lining to the inside of the bag (**C**).

Step 7

Roll the facing with your fingers so that it is not visible from the outside and pin in place all around the top, ensuring that everything sits correctly (**D**). Top-stitch through all layers, about $5/8$in (15mm) from the top of the bag. Use a long stitch length and sew cautiously through the bulkier areas. Press lightly.

If necessary, to secure the lining inside the bag further, you can also hand-stitch a few stitches at the side seams, through bag and facings. Stitch invisibly in the 'ditch' of the seam. This should not really be necessary if you have top-stitched around the top of the bag. Give the bag a final press.

Lining a bag without a facing

Line the bag in exactly the same way, except that the lining will come right to the top of the bag and the snap will be attached directly to the lining instead of the facing (**E**).

To line a bag with a back zipper opening, see instructions on setting in a zip, page 28.

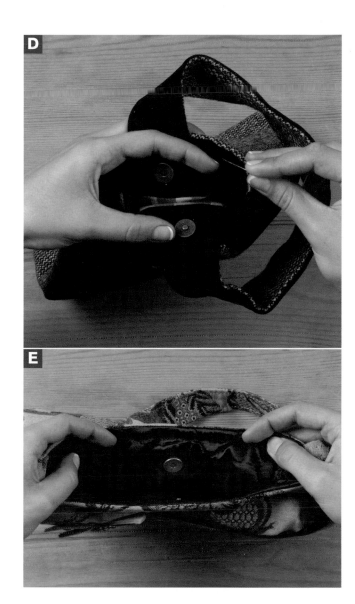

zip fasteners

Zippers provide an easy and secure closure for handbags, although traditionally they are thought to be tricky to set in neatly. The method I use in this book for setting in a zipper is neat, easier to apply and is set into the back of the bag where it is hidden from view and so doesn't detract from the look of the finished bag.

how to set in a back zipper

Back zippers are used for many of the projects in this book. Those that use this method of zip fasteners have iron-on interfaced back sections. Most projects in this book use a 7, 8 or 9in (18, 21 or 23cm) zip. A light (dress) weight zipper is suitable for lighter materials and evening bags, and a heavier zipper may be needed for canvas bags.

Step 1
Begin by ironing the interfacing onto the wrong side of the back section of your bag following the manufacturer's guidelines. You may need to press with a damp cloth to release the bonding unit in the interfacing effectively.

Step 2
Clip out the triangular zipper markers on the paper pattern piece and transfer them onto the interfaced side (reverse) of the back section of the bag using a soft pencil (**A**).

Step 3
Mark a rectangle from the top of the triangle on the left to the top of the triangle on the right, and back across from the bottom of the triangle. The rectangle will measure ¼in (6mm) by the length of your zipper (7 or 8in (18 or 21cm)). As this will not be seen, you can use a soft pencil to draw the lines onto the interfacing (**B**).

Step 4
Pin the back lining piece to the main back piece, right sides together. With the interfacing upwards, stitch along the marked rectangular zip line using a short stitch length.

Step 5
Cut through all layers very carefully up the centre of the rectangle and clip diagonally to the corners (**C**).

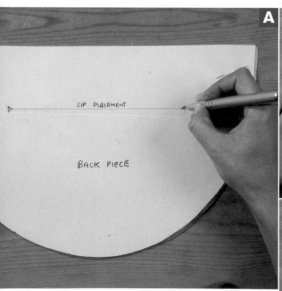
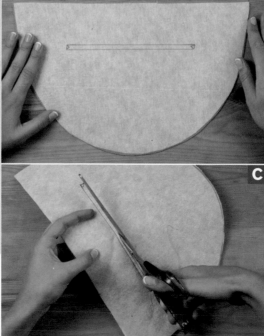
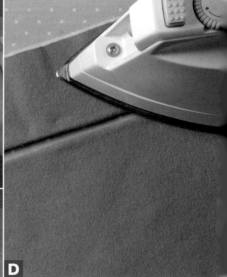

making **vintage** bags

Step 6

Turn the lining through the centre of the cut rectangle to the inside, along the stitching. It is important that the lining doesn't show obviously from the fabric side. To ensure neatness, roll the lining towards the inside with your fingers, pin and hand-baste in place (**D**). Press and then remove basting stitches.

Step 7

Whipstitch the open end of the zipper (**E**).

Step 8

Centre the zipper under the opening, right side of the fabric up and hand-baste in place (**F**).

Step 9

From the right side, edge-stitch the zipper in place around the opening. Use a zipper foot and a medium stitch length. The edge-stitching will show so take care and stitch very slowly (**G**).

Step 10

Press again using a cloth. Remember to leave the zipper **open** when you have pressed it, as the bag will be turned through it when the other lining piece has been attached.

lining a bag with a back zipper

For the designs in this book that use the back zipper fastening, you will go on to assemble the bag using the following method. Note that the main back piece is now attached to the back lining via the zipper.

Step 1

Stitch appropriate handle/carrier to bag front piece, face down and right sides together.

Step 2

Pin main front piece to back piece, right sides together and stitch around the outside edges, using a ½in (13mm) seam allowance. Leave the lining piece **free** (**A**).

Step 3

Then pin the front lining to the back lining (which is now attached to the main bag back at the zipper opening) right sides together and sew around outside edges, leaving a gap of around 5in (13cm) in the centre bottom to turn through (**B**). The hole must be large enough to get the handle through.

(continued on page 30)

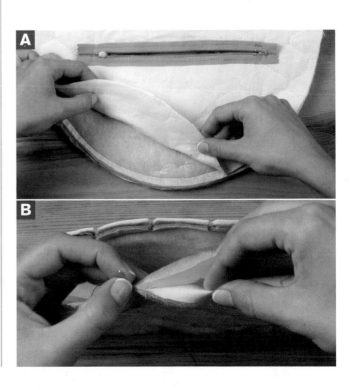

29

making **vintage** bags

Step 4

Turn the whole bag right side out through the hole in the lining and then through the open zip (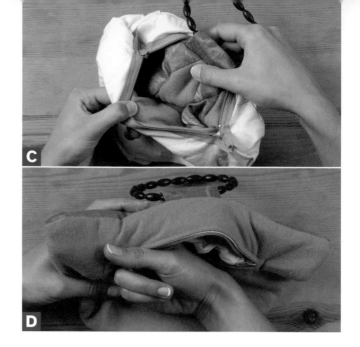**C**).

Step 5

Tuck the lining into the back. Push the corners of the bag outwards and shape curved edges with your fingers, gaining access through the gap in the lining (**D**).

Step 6

Slip-stitch the gap in the lining closed. Tuck the lining back into the bag, pushing any corners firmly into the corresponding corners of the bag. Ensure that the lining sits correctly then give the bag a press.

how to set in a top zipper

For projects where a back zipper is not appropriate, it is necessary to set a zipper into the top seam. The only difference is that with this method, you have to hand-stitch the lining inside to the zipper tape when the bag is finished.

Step 1

Stitch front and back sections of bag together at upper edges, leaving open between * marks. Baste section between the * marks (**A**). Press the seam open flat.

Step 2

With the zipper closed and face down, centre it over the basted pressed seam and baste in place

approximately ¼in (6mm) from the teeth of the zipper. You will use this basting line as a sewing guide from the other side (**B**).

Step 3

Turn bag right side up and from right side, machine stitch zipper in place. Stitch over the basting, and across top and bottom ends of zipper. You will need to use a zipper foot for this (**C**). Take out basting stitches and leave the zipper open.

After the bag has been completed, the lining is then inserted into the bag, wrong sides together, and is hand-stitched in place around the zipper tape.

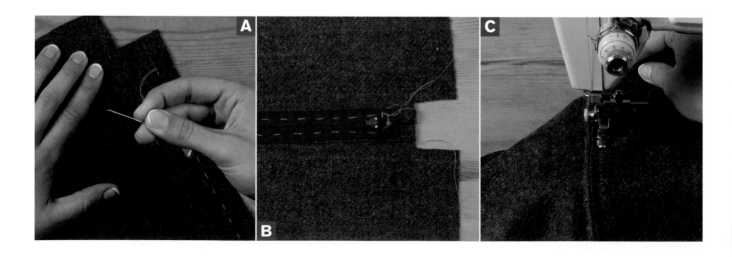

making matching purses

Some of the handbags in this book have matching
purses. In the last century, matching purses often came
included as a feature of the bag – sometimes along
with mirrors, powder boxes and perfume bottles. I've
chosen styles which I felt would be enhanced with a
harmonizing purse, but many of the other styles would
be equally good with a matching purse and the purse
pattern included below can be made to match any of
the bags by using the appropriate fabric and trimmings.

Below I have set out instructions on how to make a
basic lined purse with a zip fastener, which measures
6 x 5in (15 x 13cm) when finished (they are of a
sufficient size to be used as coin purses, make-up
purses or similar). All of the purses featured in this
book use the same basic pattern piece and are made
unique by their trims, which usually tie in with the bag.

You will need to use the Basic Purse **91** pattern
template. This uses a 6in (15cm) zipper. Cut two **91**
pieces from fabric, two from iron-on interfacing and two
from lining fabric. Trim about ½in (13mm) from the
upper edge of both lining pieces to ensure the lining is
slightly smaller than the purse and sits correctly inside.

Step 1
Iron interfacing onto wrong side of each purse **91** main
fabric section.

Step 2
Whipstitch the open end of zipper together.

Step 3
Pin the zipper to the upper edge of one purse piece,
right sides together, then using a zipper foot, stitch
approximately ⅛in (3mm) from the teeth of the zipper (**A**).

Step 4
Pin one lining piece to the upper edge of purse and
with raw edges even, stitch over previous line of
stitching (**B**). The zipper will be sandwiched between.

(continued on page 32)

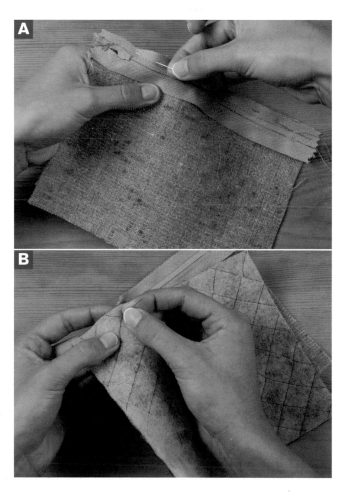

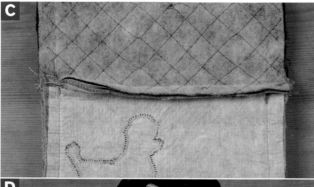

Step 5

Turn right side out and press both lining and fabric away from zipper.

Step 6

Complete the other side of the purse in the same way.

Step 7

Open zipper and place right sides of purse and lining together. Stitch around outside edge of purse, up to zipper on each side. Stitch lining up to zipper each side, leaving a gap of around 4in (10cm) in base of lining for turning (**C**).

Step 8

Turn purse right side out (**D**).

Step 9

Slip-stitch the gap in the lining and push lining to inside of purse (**E**). Close zipper and press thoroughly.

---

sewing tips

After you have turned the purse right side out, you may need to hand-stitch a few stitches on the outside of the purse at either end of the zipper tape to keep the zipper ends held together and tucked in neatly.

You can embellish your purse to match any of the bags in the book. Remember that if you are using flat appliqué, this must be applied before you stitch the purse together. Three-dimensional trims can be applied after the purse is finished.

embellishments

You can really be creative and have fun with embellishment. Trims can be fun and loud, or subtle and classy. Embellishing imaginatively is one of the best ways to give your bag a vintage feel and the essential ingredient to personalizing it and making it yours. It is fairly easy to pick up pieces of genuine vintage lace or original vintage buttons from antique or flea markets that can be used to trim your bag and give it a piece of real nostalgia. These small pieces can integrate well with modern, more durable fabrics.

Many of the vintage style trims, including bows, flowers and novelty appliqué, have enjoyed a fashion comeback in recent years. It can also be a nice idea to sew a fabric label into your bag. Apart from personalizing your work even further it can provide a professional finishing touch to a handmade bag. You can have name tape labels woven quite cheaply and in small quantities. If you have a computer and colour printer, you can make your own labels using fabric transfer paper (see section on **Photo Print Bags**, page 37).

There are two main ways of trimming the outside of your bag – flat appliqué or three-dimensional trims.

flat appliqué

Flat appliqué includes anything which must be stitched onto the relevant bag piece before the bag is assembled. This encompasses lace, braid, flat ribbon trims, novelty shapes or pictures. In the 1940s and 50s in particular, there was a trend for novelty appliqué like animals, fruit and flowers. There is no limit to the creative shapes you can apply to your own bag and you can really have fun designing them.

Several of the project bags in this book have flat appliqué which must be stitched onto the relevant bag piece (usually the front) before the bag is assembled.

how to add a flat appliqué

Step 1

First copy and cut out the template for the relevant appliqué. (I am using the sausage dog appliqué here to demonstrate the basic technique.) Cut out a square of the appliqué fabric, slightly larger than the shape template and cut a piece of fusible web (Bondaweb for example) the same size as the fabric. Iron the fusible web onto the back of the fabric, paper side up, following the manufacturer's guidelines.

Step 2

Turn the template over and draw round it with a soft pen onto the paper backing of the fusible web (**A**). You need to reverse the image because the finished appliqué will be the other way around as you are drawing onto the back of the fusible web.

Step 3

Cut very carefully around the drawn shape using appliqué or other sharp scissors (**B**).
Peel the paper backing off the shape.

Step 4

Place the appliqué on the right side of the relevant bag/purse piece where you want it to be, and then fuse the appliqué into place using an iron and following the manufacturer's instructions. Always interface the piece that you are stitching the appliqué onto first – this will stabilize the fabric and prevent stretching or distortion.

Step 5

Next, you will need to machine stitch the appliqué shape all around the outside edge using a 'satin stitch'. This is where the machine is set to a zigzag stitch with a narrow/medium width (2–5mm wide) and a short stitch length. This will result in close stitches. It may be wise to experiment on a spare scrap of fabric to get the stitch as you want it before starting on the appliqué. Use a regular zigzag foot. The raw edge of the appliqué should be positioned under the centre right of the foot, so that when the needle swings to the far right on zigzag, it comes over the edge of the appliqué onto the fabric and encases the raw edge of the appliqué within the stitches.

Stitch very slowly and carefully, especially around the corners and small areas. For corners, sew past the corner a little way and with needle down in the fabric, pivot the fabric and stitch over the previous few stitches before proceeding.

Step 6

Apply any additional decoration to the appliqué. Adding beads and ribbons is much easier at this stage while the piece is flat, before you have assembled and lined the bag/purse.

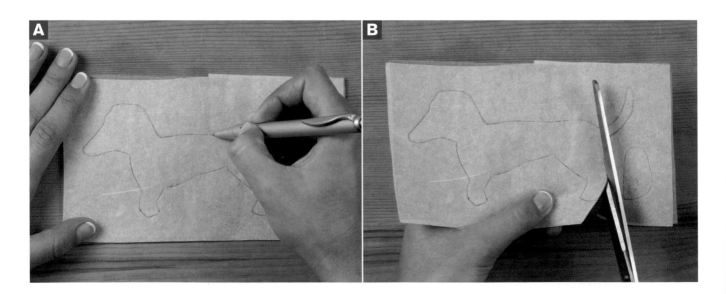

three-dimensional trims

Three-dimensional appliqué includes anything which can be hand-stitched onto the bag after the main structure has been completed. This covers bows, ribbon or fabric flowers, feathers, fluffy braids and buttons. There is a wonderful choice of modern braids on the market today and haberdashery has enjoyed renewed interest. Take time to search out something different to trim your bag with – you'll be surprised at what you can find. You can also make your own trims – many of the projects in the book have handmade three-dimensional trims, often quite pronounced, which make a real statement.

making a bow
style 1: angled bow

Bow style 1 is a floppy bow with angled corners. It is used for **Patricia** and **Vivien** (pages 102 and 116). You will need two pattern pieces – main bow and bow centre. Cut two main bow pieces and one bow centre piece from your chosen bow fabric.

Step 1
Pin two main bow pieces right sides together. Stitch around the outside edge, leaving an opening between * and *, for turning the bow to the right side. Use a seam allowance of ½in (13mm) (**A**).

Step 2
Trim seams back to ¼in (6mm), clip corners and turn right side out. Hand slip-stitch opening closed (**B**).

Step 3
Gather or pleat along centre line of bow using large hand-gathering stitches. Pull up gathers/pleats and secure with several overhand stitches (**C**).

(continued on page 36)

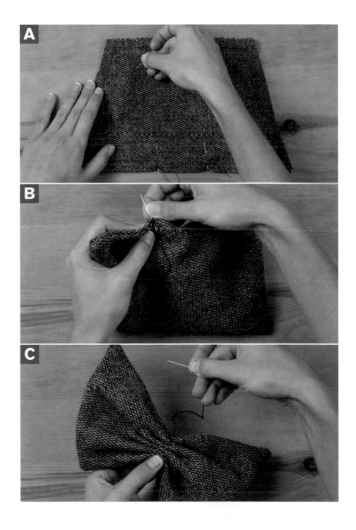

Step 4

Iron fusible web to wrong side of bow centre piece. Peel off paper backing, turn long edges of piece in so that they meet in the middle, then press with a cloth (**D**).

Step 5

Stitch short ends together to form a short tube and turn the tube right side out (**E**).

Step 6

Slide tube over the bow and position it in the middle, covering the gathers (**F**). Hand tack centre in place from behind.

style 2: rounded bow

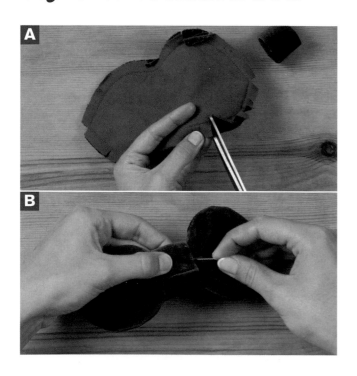

This alternative style is a neat rounded bow with curved edges. It is used for **Dorothy** and **Peggy** (pages 52 and 124). You will need two pattern pieces – main bow and bow centre. Cut two main bow pieces and one bow centre piece from your chosen bow fabric.

This bow is assembled in the same way as Style 1: Angled Bow, but you will have to clip the curved seam allowance and the corners, before turning (**A**).

Tack the bow centre in place from behind, as for the Angled Bow (**B**).

ribbon roses

Some of the bags in this book are trimmed with ribbon roses, made using the 'twist and fold' method. It took me some time to get the hang of this, but perseverance is well worthwhile as there are so many bags which can be brought to life with blooms of this kind. They can also double as corsage brooches and as there are so many beautiful ribbons on the market (including some vintage), there is no limit to the variations you can make.

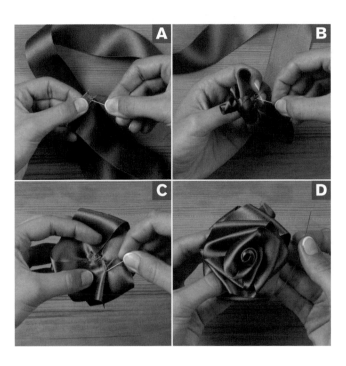

Step 1

Take a length of 1½in (38mm) width ribbon approximately 32in (82cm) long. Roll one end over about three or four times to form a centre. Hand-stitch through all layers at the base of the rose (**A**).

Step 2

The ribbon must then be twisted spirally and secured with stitches at the base each time it is folded. Make certain that you sew through all of the layers each time, to ensure that the folds are firmly fixed in place (**B**).

Step 3

Once a rose of the required size is achieved, cut off remaining ribbon, fold the raw edge under and stitch in place (**C**), (**D**).

photo print bags

One of the projects in this book uses a photo transfer. There are a few different ways in which you can acheive this effect. If you have a computer and a colour printer, you can scan in a photo or sketch, reverse the image within your printer settings and print it with your inkjet printer onto special transfer paper that is now widely available. The package will give instructions on how to use the transfer paper, but it usually involves trimming the transfer down with scissors, placing it onto a piece of plain cotton (or other natural fibre plain fabric) and ironing over the back of the transfer for between one and four minutes. When it has cooled, peel off the backing paper carefully and the image will stay on the fabric. This can then be stitched to your bag piece and the raw edges can be turned in or covered with ribbon or braid. (See **Gloria**, page 130).

If you don't have computer facilities, you can take a chosen photograph or image to a colour copy shop where they can make a colour photocopy that can then be transferred to fabric using a special transfer medium (gel). Again this is a specialist area and there are lots of transfer products on the market. You can find out more about each product by reading the individual instructions. It is also helpful to talk to the manufacturers or to staff at craft shops.

If you don't have access to either of these, you can cut a 'picture' out of a fabric that has a large print, for example a 'scene' from a piece of 'Toile du Jouey' fabric or a single large flower. This can be stitched to your bag piece and then 'framed' in the same way as the photo transfers with ribbon or braid.

1920s

clara

1920s TWO-TONE ART DECO POCKET BAG

This bag draws inspiration from the flat simple shape of the beaded cloth and mesh purses of the early 1920s. The long geometric silhouette and panelled appliqué also echo the Art Deco styling of the period.

The handbag as we know it today has only been in existence for a relatively short period – before this, ladies carried only the bare essentials in small pocket-style reticules.

This bag is just large enough to house the modern-day essentials and the decorative beaded handles are practical for slipping over the wrist, making this an ideal bag for evening wear.

dimensions

Approximately 9in (23cm) deep by 9in (23cm) wide (excluding handles)

pattern pieces

1 **2** **3** page 134

suggested fabrics

for main bag fabric:
cotton-backed fake suede or velveteen (which can be ironed)

for bag lining:
firm weight plain or patterned silks

for appliqué:
silk brocade and velvet ribbon

you will need

* 14in (36cm) of fake suede for main bag, 36in (92cm) wide

* 14in (36cm) of firm weight iron-on interfacing, 36in (92cm) wide

* 14in (36cm) of firm weight silk fabric for lining, 36in (92cm) wide

* 6 x 12in (15 x 31cm) square of patterned silk brocade for appliqué strip

* 6 x 12in (15 x 31cm) square of fusible web for appliqué

* Piece of ¾in (18mm) wide ribbon, 24in (62cm) long, for edging appliqué

* 2 pieces x 1½in (4cm) square of craft interfacing (for snap stabilizers)

* 1 magnetic snap set

* 28in (72cm) of hobby wire for handles in 1.2mm or 16 gauge

* Approximately 36 oval wooden beads (with large holes) size 8 x 16mm (18 per handle)

cutting out

* Cut 2 x piece **1** (front/back) from main fabric

* Cut 2 x piece **1** (front/back) from iron-on interfacing

* Cut 2 x piece **1** (front/back) from lining fabric

* Cut 1 x piece **2** (appliqué strip) from patterned brocade

* Cut 1 x piece **2** (appliqué strip) from fusible web

* Cut 2 x piece **3** (handle carrier) from main fabric

* Cut 2 x piece **3** (handle carrier) from fusible web

* Cut 2 lengths of ribbon, 12in (31cm) long

making up instructions

Step 1
Cut the wire coil in two and make a pair of beaded ring handles, using 18 beads per handle. Refer to **Beaded Ring Handles**, page 22.

Step 2
Iron interfacing pieces **1** to corresponding front and back sections **1** following manufacturer's guidelines.

Step 3
Iron fusible web piece **2** onto appliqué strip piece **2**. Remove paper backing, position appliqué right side up centrally, on right side of front bag piece (following marking lines on pattern) and fuse into place through a cloth (**A**).

Pin a strip of velvet ribbon down each side of appliqué (**B**), covering the raw edges of the central appliqué strip on both sides. Stitch in place down both edges of each ribbon strip. Press lightly from the wrong side using a damp cloth.

Step 4
Pin the two interfaced front/back pieces together, right sides together. Stitch around side and lower edges, leaving a ½in (13mm) seam allowance. Clip seam allowance at corners (**C**) and turn right side out.

Step 5
Iron fusible web onto wrong sides of both handle carrier pieces **3**. Peel off paper backing, turn in edges marked with a dotted line on pattern piece to centre and fuse in place. Refer to **Self-fabric Handles**, page 20.

Step 6
Fold a handle carrier around each beaded ring handle (**D**) and machine-baste along the bottom edge, about ½in (13mm) from raw edges. Secure each handle in place by making a few hand-stitches either side of each handle carrier. Ensure that the stitches are tight up against the beads to stop the

handles from sliding round and showing the join in the wire.

Step 7
Pin one handle carrier to the bag front and one to the back centrally (**E**) and machine-baste to bag over the previous row of basting.

Step 8
Transfer magnetic snap placement markers onto the front and back lining pieces **1**, and fix magnetic snap. Refer to **Magnetic Snaps**, page 24. Remember to use a snap stabilizer as the snaps are fixed to the lining fabric and this will need extra support. Also, if you are using a label, it is at this point that you should stitch it to the back lining of the bag.

Step 9
Stitch lining pieces together around sides and lower edges, but leave a gap of around 5in (13cm) in the centre of the bottom edge, for turning the bag through.

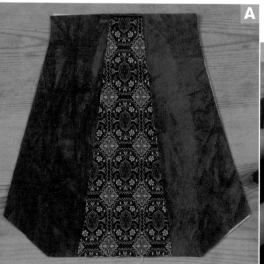

NB: The hole must be big enough for you to get the handles through!

Step 10

With right sides together, pin the lining to the bag through all thicknesses (including handle carriers) ensuring that the upper edges are even (**F**). Stitch slowly and carefully through all thicknesses using a medium stitch length and leaving a seam allowance of ½in (13mm). Clip into seam allowance round side seams.

Step 11

Turn the bag right side out through the opening in the bottom of the lining and slip-stitch the opening closed. Refer to the section on **Basic Stitches**, page 12. Turn the lining into the bag.

Step 12

Roll the lining with your fingers so that it is not visible from the outside, pin and hand-baste it in

variations

If you don't want to make beaded **handles**, you can substitute **gilt metal rings** (which can be purchased from craft stores) or ready-made **plastic circular** bag handles. Those with a 'tortoise shell' coloured finish look quite vintage, especially when used with muted-shade fabrics. For this size bag, use ring handles with a maximum diameter of 4in (10cm).

This project uses **fake suede**, which is much easier to work with, and care for, than real suede. Fake suede has many advantages. Ultrasuede in the USA for example has a sueded finish on both sides, a very soft handle and it doesn't fray, making it ideal also for appliqué. The **cotton backed** or **stretch** varieties of fake suede handle more like fabric. The advantage of these is that they can usually be ironed and washed.

place around upper edge of bag. Top-stitch through all layers, about ½in (13mm) from the top of the bag, using a long stitch length. Do up snap, and then give the bag a final light press.

43

clara

1920s

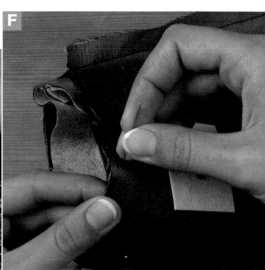

making **vintage** bags

lucille

1920s MINI EVENING BAG WITH RIBBON ROSE

This cute evening bag uses a bracelet as a handle and is trimmed with a two-tone ribbon rose and feather leaves. It follows the basic flat shape of 1920s clutch bags, but the asymmetric flap and ring handle give it a different character.

The use of a bangle for a handle is a novel idea, and this bag is so small and neat, you can actually carry it on your wrist. The fluffy marabou feathers, toning ribbon for the rose and the rich velvet are evocative of vintage styles – this little bag would have made the perfect cocktail party accessory for the stylish 1920s flapper girl.

dimensions

Approximately 6in (15cm) deep by 10in (26cm) wide (excluding handle)

pattern pieces

4 **5** **6** **7** **8**

pages 135–6

suggested fabrics

for main bag fabric:
cotton velvet

for bag lining:
firm weight plain or patterned silks

you will need

* 14in (36cm) of main fabric, 36in (92cm) wide

* 8in (21cm) of lining fabric, 36in (92cm) wide

* 9in (23cm) of sew-in craft interfacing fabric, 36in (92cm) wide

* 4 x 5in (10 x 13cm) of fusible web for handle carrier

* 9 x 9in (23 x 23cm) of iron-on interfacing for flap

* one plastic or metal bangle for bag handle

* 32in (82cm) of two-tone ribbon, 1½in (38mm) width for rose trim

* three short marabou feathers

* two pieces x 1½in (4cm) square of craft interfacing (for snap stabilizers)

* one magnetic snap set

cutting out

* Cut 2 x piece **4** (front/back) from main fabric

* Cut 2 x piece **4** (front/back) from sew-in craft interfacing

* Cut 2 x piece **5** (front/back facing) from main fabric

* Cut 2 x piece **6** (front/back lining) from lining fabric

* Cut 2 x piece **7** (flap) from main fabric

* Cut 2 x piece **7** (flap) from iron on interfacing

* Cut 1 x piece **8** (handle carrier) from main fabric and from fusible web

making up instructions

Step 1

Pin front and back **4** sections to corresponding front and back interfacing sections **4** and baste together. Refer to **Using Sew-in Interfacing**, page 17.

Step 2

Make one interfaced section your bag front. Transfer magnetic snap placement marker onto bag front piece and fix magnetic section of snap. Refer to **Magnetic Snaps**, page 24.

Step 3

Pin the two interfaced front/back pieces together, right sides of main fabric together. Stitch around side and lower edges, leaving a ½in (13mm) seam allowance. Clip seam allowance at corners and curved edge and turn bag right side out.

Step 4

Iron fusible web onto wrong side of handle carrier piece **8**. Peel off paper backing, turn in edges marked with a dotted line on pattern piece to centre and fuse in place. Refer to **Self-fabric handles**, page 20.

Step 5

Fold the handle carrier around the bangle handle and machine-baste bottom edges together, about ½in (13mm) from raw edges.
NB: Depending on how thick the bangle is, you may have to trim a little from the bottom of the handle carrier. The basting should be fairly close to the handle.

Step 6

Pin the handle carrier to the bag front piece at centre point, having raw edges even. Baste to bag over the previous row of basting (**A**).

Step 7

Make flap. Iron interfacing onto both flap pieces **7**. Take the bottom piece of the flap, transfer snap marker and fix other half of magnetic snap (**B**). Then with right sides together, pin and stitch top and bottom flap pieces together at sides and lower edges, leaving top straight edge open. Turn right side out and top-stitch ¼in (6mm) from finished edge.

Step 8

Baste and stitch the flap to the bag back at centre point, having raw edges even (**C**).

Step 9

Stitch lower edge of facing pieces **5** to upper edge of lining pieces **6**, having right sides together. Refer to **How to Line a Top-opening Bag**, on page 26.

Step 10

Stitch lining/facing pieces together down sides and along bottom edge, leaving a gap of around 5in (13cm) in the centre of the bottom for turning the bag through.

Step 11

Insert bag into lining, right sides together. Pin lining and bag together at upper edges, with raw edges even. You will be pinning through the flap and handle carrier also. Stitch through all thicknesses. Note that this will be quite a lot of thicknesses to sew through and as the bag is small, you will need to stitch slowly and carefully. Trim the seam back to around ⅜in (1cm) to eliminate bulk, and clip into seam allowance at sides.

Step 12

Turn the bag through the opening in the lining and temporarily push the lining to the inside of the bag. Refer to **How to Line a Top-opening Bag**, page 26. Roll the facing with your fingers so that it is not visible from the outside and pin it in place around the top, ensuring that the flap and handle sit correctly. Hand-baste around top edge. Top-stitch through all

layers, about ½in (13mm) from top edge of bag, using a long stitch length. Again, this will be quite a lot of thicknesses to sew through, so stitch slowly and carefully. Press.

Step 13

Slip-stitch the opening in the lining closed, tuck lining into bag and give the bag a final press with a cloth. Refer to **Basic Stitches**, page 12.

Step 14

Make a 'folded rose' using two-tone ribbon referring to **Ribbon Roses**, page 37.

Step 15

Gather and tie the feathers together with double thread attached to a needle (**D**) and stitch to left front of bag in a leaf arrangement. Position rose over quill ends of feathers and hand-sew in place (**E**).

For small bags like this one, bangles make a perfect option for a handle. It is very easy to pick up plastic bangles in fashion shops. They often have quite a retro look and come in a much better range of colours than purpose-made bag handles. It is also possible to find bangles in unusual shapes like squares or triangles. Metal bangles are another possibility, but as they are often quite thin, consider using several together. The bag can then be worn dangling from the wrist – a feature of early 1900s vintage bags.

lucille

47

1900s

making **vintage** bags

virginia

1920s MINI CLUTCH WITH TASSEL AND RIBBON ROSE

This bag uses the same basic pattern pieces as the previous project (Lucille), with the addition of a different asymmetric flap and a neat self-fabric handle. The 1920s theme is echoed in the decorative stitching detail on the front of the bag. The tassel trim and the grosgrain rose also add to the period feel.

This is a small bag which can be made up in plain fake suede fabrics for smart day wear or in silk fabrics for evening wear. The use of one colour – mocha chocolate or tan for example – for the fabric, tassel and ribbon gives uniformity while showing a variety of different textures.

you will need

* 16in (41cm) of main fabric, 48in (122cm) wide

* 8in (21cm) of lining fabric, 36in (92cm) wide

* 9in (23cm) of sew-in craft interfacing fabric, 36in (92cm) wide

* 2 x 18in (6 x 46cm) exactly of fusible web for handle

* 32in (82cm) of matching grosgrain ribbon, 1½in (38mm) width for rose trim

* one matching tassel (with loop top)

* two pieces x 1½in (4cm) square of craft interfacing (for snap stabilizers)

* one magnetic snap set

cutting out

* Cut 2 x piece **9** (front/back) from main fabric

* Cut 2 x piece **9** (front/back) from sew-in craft interfacing

* Cut 2 x piece **10** (front/back facing) from main fabric

* Cut 2 x piece **11** (front/back lining) from lining fabric

* Cut 2 x piece **12** (flap) from main fabric

* Cut 1 x piece **12** (flap) from sew-in craft interfacing

* Cut 1 x piece **13** (handle) from main fabric and fusible web on fold

dimensions

Approximately 6in (15cm) deep by 10½in (27cm) wide (excluding handle)

pattern pieces

9 **10** **11** **12** **13**

pages 137–8

suggested fabrics

for main bag fabric:
fake suede

for bag lining:
firm weight plain or patterned silks

virginia

49

1920s

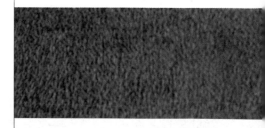

making up instructions

Step 1

Pin front and back **9** sections to corresponding front and back **9** interfacing sections and baste together. Refer to **Using Sew-in Interfacing**, page 17.

Step 2

Make one interfaced section your bag front. Transfer magnetic snap placement marker onto bag front piece and fix magnetic section of snap. Refer to **Magnetic Snaps**, page 24. Transfer decorative stitching lines from pattern template onto interfaced side of bag front. Do this by marking top and bottom points of lines with tailor's tacks and then drawing onto interfacing using a soft pencil. Stitch down the lines using a medium to long stitch length (**A**).

Step 3

Pin the two interfaced front/back pieces together, right sides of main fabric together. Stitch around side and lower edges, leaving a ½in

(13mm) seam allowance. Clip into seam allowance at corners and curved edge, and turn bag right side out.

Step 4

Make flap. Baste interfacing to the bottom piece of the flap **12** only. Transfer snap marker and fix other half of magnetic snap. Then with right sides together, pin and stitch top and bottom flap pieces together at two lower edges, leaving top straight edge open. Turn and top-stitch ¼in (6mm) from edge (**B**).

Step 5

Make handle. Iron fusible web onto the wrong side of the handle **13** piece. Fold the long edges into the centre and fuse them in place. Fold in half lengthways again. Machine stitch open edges together about ¼in (6mm) from the open edge. Press. Refer to the section on **Self-fabric Handles**, page 20.

Step 6

Pin the finished flap onto the back of the bag, right outside of flap against right outside of bag back, and with raw edges even (**C**). Stitch using a long stitch length, approximately ½in (13mm) from the edge.

Step 7

Thread the tassel onto the handle and on outside of bag, positioned next to flap and centred over side seams with raw edges even, pin the handle to the bag and baste in place (**D**).

Step 8

Stitch lower edge of facing pieces **10** to upper edge of lining pieces **11**, having right sides together. Refer to **How to Line a Top-opening Bag**, page 26.

Step 9

Stitch lining/facing pieces together at sides and lower edges, leaving a gap of around 5in (13cm) in the

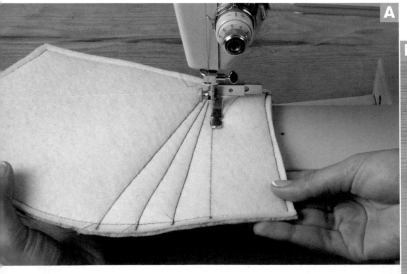

making **vintage** bags

centre of the bottom. You will turn the bag through this gap later

Step 10

Insert the bag into the lining, right sides together. Pin lining and bag together at upper edges, having raw edges even. You will be pinning through the flap and handle also. Stitch through all thicknesses. Note that this will be quite a lot of thicknesses to sew through and as the bag is small, you will need to stitch slowly and carefully. Trim the seam back to around ⅜in (1cm) to eliminate bulk, and clip into seam allowance at sides.

Step 11

Turn the bag through the opening in the lining and push the lining temporarily to the inside of the bag. Refer to **How to Line a Top-opening Bag**, page 26. Roll the facing with your fingers so that it is not visible from the outside and pin it in place around the top, ensuring that the flap and handle

sit correctly. Hand-baste around top edge. Top-stitch through all layers, about ½in (13mm) from the top edge of the bag, using a long stitch length. Again, this will be quite a lot of thicknesses to sew through, so stitch slowly and carefully. Press.

Step 12

Slip-stitch the opening in the lining, tuck lining back into bag and give the bag a final press with a cloth. Refer to **Basic Stitches**, page 12.

Step 13

Make a 'folded rose' using grosgrain ribbon. Refer to **Ribbon Roses**, page 37.

Step 14

Position rose on left front of bag, at top of decorative stitching, low enough to avoid flap. Hand-sew in place. Position tassel on right-hand side of bag handle (**E**).

The decorative stitching on the front of this bag should be done from the interfacing side. Remember to transfer the lines onto the opposite (right-hand) side of the piece, as they will be reversed when you turn the piece right (fabric) side up.

This pattern of lines was very characteristic of Art Deco designs of the 1920s. This kind of stitching can take on a three-dimensional quilted effect if you sandwich a thin layer of wadding between the fabric and interfacing pieces.

virginia

51

1920s

making **vintage** bags

dorothy

1920s ASYMMETRIC BOW FLAP CLUTCH BAG

This bag design is inspired by the 'clutch' bags of the late 1920s – simple envelope-style bags which were originally known as 'pochette' bags. Clutch bags are designed to be held in the hand or tucked under the arm. Because of the simple, elegant shape of the clutch bag, 1920s and 30s designers often embossed or decorated it with unusual trims including jewelled, lucite or Bakelite clasps and frames.

dimensions

Approximately 7in (18cm) deep by 11½in (29cm) wide (excluding handle)

pattern pieces

14 **15** **16** **17**

pages 139–40

suggested fabrics

for main bag fabric:
wool/tweed

for bag lining:
patterned silks

for bow:
short pile velvet

This small, neat bag is of simple construction in the style of its 20th century predecessors. It owes its elegance to the striking asymmetric flap (very popular in the late 20s and early 30s) and single large velvet bow, stitched on at a jaunty angle.

The simplicity of the design makes it ideal for smart day wear made up in a wool tweed fabric, or stunning for evening wear in silk brocade. Variations could include omitting the bow and replacing it with a single large original vintage button.

you will need

* 12in (31cm) of main fabric, 54in (140cm) wide
* 12in (31cm) of lining fabric, 36in (92cm) wide
* 18in (46cm) of sew-in craft interfacing, 36in (92cm) wide
* one piece of velvet 9in (23cm) deep x 18in (46cm) wide for the bow
* 2 x 4in (6 x 10cm) exactly of fusible web for bow centre
* two pieces of craft interfacing 1½in (4cm) square of craft interfacing (for snap stabilizers)
* one magnetic snap set

cutting out

* Cut 2 x piece **14** (front/back) from main fabric
* Cut 2 x piece **14** (front/back) from lining fabric
* Cut 2 x piece **14** (front/back) from sew-in craft interfacing
* Cut 2 x piece **15** (flap) from main fabric (cut with wrong sides together)
* Cut 1 x piece **15** (flap) from craft interfacing
* Cut 2 x piece **16** (bow) from velvet (wrong sides together and on cross grain)
* Cut 1 x piece **17** (bow centre) from velvet
* Cut 1 x piece **17** (bow centre) from fusible web

Step 1

Pin front and back sections **14** to corresponding front and back interfacing sections **14** and baste together. Refer to **Using Sew-in Interfacing**, page 17.

Step 2

Lay the two flap fabric pieces **15** wrong sides together, in front of you with the 'tab' facing towards the right. Take the top layer off and lay the interfacing piece **15** on top of (on the wrong side of) remaining flap piece. Pin together and stitch all around, ¼in (6mm) from outside edge, securing interfacing to bottom flap piece on all sides. Transfer the magnetic snap position marker onto interfacing side of the flap and fix non-magnetic half of snap (**A**). Refer to **Magnetic Snaps**, page 24.

Step 3

Now pin the remaining flap section to the interfaced flap section, right sides together. Stitch together round curved side/lower edges, leaving a ½in (13mm) seam allowance. Trim away any excess bulk, clip into the seam allowance round curves and turn right sides out. Press flat with a damp cloth, then top-stitch all around using a longer stitch length. Press again.

Step 4

Make one interfaced section your bag front. Transfer the magnetic snap placement marker onto the bag front piece and fix magnetic section of snap (**B**).

Step 5

Pin the two interfaced front/back pieces together, right sides of main fabric together. Stitch together around sides and lower edges, leaving a ½in (13mm) seam allowance. Trim seams back to ⅜in (1cm) to reduce bulk. Insert finger into a bottom corner. Match up the seam on the bottom and side, pin through all thicknesses (**C**) and stitch straight across the corner to form a gusset. Clip off corners of gusset leaving ½in (13mm) seam allowance (**D**).

Step 6

Repeat this on the opposite corner. Turn bag right sides out and press.

Step 7

Pin the finished flap onto the back of the bag, right outside of flap against right outside of bag back, with raw edges even. Baste using a long stitch length, approximately ½in (13mm) from the edge.

Step 8

Stitch lining pieces together at side and lower edges, leaving a gap of around 5in (13cm) in the centre of the bottom to turn the bag through. Insert your finger into one of the bottom corners. Match up seam on bottom and side, pin through all thicknesses and stitch straight across the corner to form a gusset as for the main bag pieces (**E**). Repeat on opposite corner.

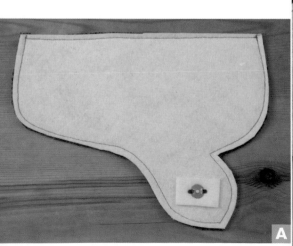

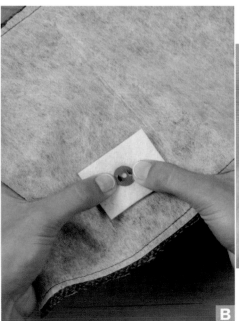

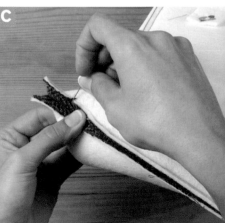

Step 9

Insert bag into lining with right sides together. Pin bag and lining together through all thicknesses round upper edges, having raw edges even. **NB: You will be pinning through the flap on the back piece too.** Stitch through all thicknesses using a normal stitch length and leaving a seam allowance of just over ½in (13mm). Note that this will be quite a lot of thicknesses to sew through, so stitch slowly and carefully. Trim seam back to ⅜in (1cm) and clip into the seam allowance at sides.

Step 10

Turn the bag through the opening in the bottom of the lining and push the lining to the inside of the bag. Refer to **How to Line a Top-opening Bag**, page 26. Roll the facing with your fingers so that it is not visible from the outside and pin in place all round top, ensuring that the flap will sit correctly. Top-stitch through all layers, about ½in (13mm) from the top, using a long stitch length. This will be quite a lot of thicknesses to sew through, so stitch slowly and carefully.

Step 11

Slip-stitch the opening in the lining closed, tuck lining back into bag and give the bag a final press with a cloth. Press first with flap open and then again with flap closed. If necessary, to secure the lining into the bag further, you can hand-stitch a few stitches at the side seams, through bag and lining.

Step 12

Construct the bow. Refer to **Making a Bow (Style 2 – Rounded Bow)**, page 36.

Step 13

Hand-stitch bow in place on flap so that it is sitting diagonally along the 'tab' on the flap as shown. Hand-stitch invisibly along top and bottom of bow band, leaving ends of bow free (**F**).

sewing tip

The bow on this style is made from velvet. Velvet has a tendency to 'walk' a little when stitched on a sewing machine. It is helpful to pin at right angles to the seam – the pins can be left in while sewing if great care is taken and this will help prevent walking.

variations

This bag makes a fantastic evening purse when made entirely (including bow) out of firm woven patterned silk brocade. If you want a less dressy clutch bag for day use, try making the entire bag in corduroy, or plain wool.

dorothy

55

1920s

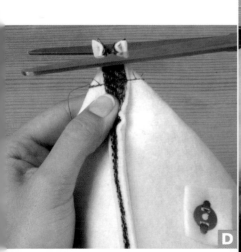

making **vintage** bags

evelyn

1920s ASYMMETRIC CLUTCH WITH VINTAGE BUTTONS

This clutch bag is made using the same pattern pieces as the previous project. However, instead of tucking the bag under-arm as you would have in the 1920s, I have added a rope handle, which allows the bag to rest on the shoulder and sit comfortably under the arm. This is more practical for modern-day use.

I've also trimmed this bag with a row of very simple vintage buttons – very popular in current fashions and a way of including a little piece of history in your modern vintage bag. Although these buttons are old, they are not particularly fancy. The fact that they once adorned a cardigan or shirt means that there are several of them, and it is the number of buttons, stitched on at an angle down the flap, which finishes this bag off with a flourish. I've made this bag in a striking piece of English woven silk brocade which makes it ideal for evening wear. It would look equally stylish made up in corduroy for day wear with a self-fabric handle.

dimensions

Approximately 7in (18cm) deep by 11½in (29cm) wide (excluding handle)

pattern pieces

18 **19** page 139–140

suggested fabrics

for main bag fabric:
silk brocade

for bag lining:
plain silk (firm weight)

you will need

* 12in (31cm) of main fabric, 54in (140cm) wide

* 18in (46cm) of sew-in craft interfacing, 36in (92cm) wide

* 12in (31cm) of lining fabric, 36in (92cm) wide

* 26in (66cm) of cord/rope for handle

* five medium-sized vintage buttons for decoration

* two pieces of craft interfacing (for snap stabilizers) 1½in (4cm) square

* one magnetic snap set

cutting out

* Cut 2 x piece **18** (front/back) from main fabric

* Cut 2 x piece **18** (front/back) from craft interfacing

* Cut 2 x piece **18** (front/back) from lining fabric

* Cut 2 x piece **19** (flap) from main fabric (cut with wrong sides together)

* Cut 1 x piece **19** (flap) from craft interfacing

making up instructions

Step 1

Pin the front and back ⑱ sections to corresponding front and back interfacing sections ⑱ and baste-stitch together. Refer to **Using Sew-in Interfacing**, page 17.

Step 2

Lay the two flap fabric pieces ⑲ wrong sides together, in front of you with the 'tab' facing towards the right. Take top layer off and lay the interfacing piece ⑲ on top of (the wrong side of) the remaining flap piece. Pin together and stitch all around, ¼in (6mm) from outside edge, securing interfacing to bottom flap piece on all sides. Transfer the magnetic snap position marker onto the interfacing side of the flap and fix the non-magnetic half of the snap. Refer to section on **Magnetic Snaps**, page 24.

Step 3

Now pin the remaining flap section to the interfaced flap section, right sides together. Stitch together

around curved side/lower edges, leaving a ½in (13mm) seam allowance. Trim away any excess bulk, clip into the seam allowance around curves and turn right sides out. Press flat with a damp cloth, then top-stitch all around using a long stitch length. Press again.

Step 4

Make one interfaced section your bag front. Transfer magnetic snap placement marker onto bag front piece and fix magnetic section.

Step 5

Pin the two interfaced front/back pieces together, right sides of main fabric together. Stitch around sides and lower edges, leaving a ½in (13mm) seam allowance. Trim the seam back to ⅜in (1cm) to cut down on bulk. Insert your finger into one of the bottom corners. Match up seam on bottom and side, pin through all thicknesses and stitch straight across the corner to form a gusset.

Step 6

Repeat this on the opposite corner. Turn bag right sides out and press.

Step 7

Pin the finished flap onto the back of the bag (**A**), right outside of flap against right outside of bag back, with raw edges even. Stitch using a long stitch length, about ½in (13mm) from the edge.

Step 8

On outside, positioned next to flap and centred over side seams with raw edges even, pin cord handle to bag (**B**) and hand-baste in place.

Step 9

Stitch lining pieces together at sides and lower edges, leaving an opening of around 5in (13cm) at centre of lower edge for turning. Insert your finger into one of the bottom corners. Match up seam on bottom and side, pin through all thicknesses and stitch straight

across the corner to form a gusset as you did for the main bag pieces. Repeat this on the opposite corner.

Step 10

With right sides together, insert bag into lining. Pin lining to bag and baste together around upper edges. Pin and baste through all thicknesses, including flap and cord handles (**C**). Stitch through all thicknesses using a normal stitch length, and leaving a little over $\frac{1}{2}$in (13mm) seam allowance. Note that this will be a lot of layers to sew through, so stitch slowly and carefully, especially over the cord. Trim the seam back to $\frac{3}{8}$in (1cm) to eliminate bulk. Clip into seam allowance at sides.

Step 11

Turn the bag right side out through the opening in the bottom of the lining and slip-stitch the opening closed. Refer to **Basic Stitches**, page 12. Then turn the lining into the bag.

Step 12

Roll the lining with your fingers so that it is not visible from the outside, pin and hand-baste it in place around upper edge of bag. Top-stitch through all layers, a little over $\frac{1}{2}$in (13mm) from the top of the bag, using a long stitch length and taking extra care when sewing through the bulkier areas (**D**). Close the flap and then give a final light press.

Step 13

Lay out your buttons on the flap. I have stitched my buttons on 1in (25mm) apart, following the diagonal of the flap. Hand-stitch in place when you are happy with your arrangement (**E**).

1930s

doris

1930s TIE HANDLE BAG WITH ROSE CORSAGE

This bag is based on a shape I found in a late 1930s mail order catalogue, billed as 'the new over-arm bag'. It features pretty tie handles which give the impression of a large soft bow. I've changed the shape, extended the handles and added magnetic closures to bring the bag up to date.

Although this floral fabric is retro and fancy enough in its own right, I've added a detachable rose corsage, made from ribbon matched to shades in the print. The vintage-style corsage can also be worn on a cardigan or jacket to tie in with the bag. This is a truly 1930s-inspired project.

you will need

✳ 20in (51cm) of main fabric, 48in (122cm) wide

✳ 14in (36cm) of lining fabric, 36in (92cm) wide

✳ 14in (36cm) of wadding, 36in (92cm) wide

✳ two pieces of craft interfacing (for snap stabilizers) 1½in (4cm) square

✳ one magnetic snap set

✳ one piece of plastic canvas to insert in base 8¼ x 2in (21 x 6cm)

cutting out

✳ Cut 2 x piece **20** (front/back) from main fabric on fold

✳ Cut 2 x piece **21** (front/back lining) from wadding on fold

✳ Cut 2 x piece **21** (front/back lining) from quilted lining fabric on fold

✳ Cut 2 x piece **22** (handle) from main fabric on fold

dimensions

Approximately 9½in (24cm) deep by 10½in (27cm) wide (excluding handle)

pattern pieces

20 **21** **22** pages 141–2

suggested fabrics

for main bag fabric:
floral printed cotton (medium weight)

for bag lining:
quilted lining fabric

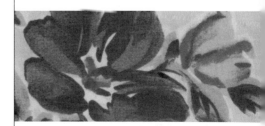

making up instructions

Step 1
Transfer pleat lines from pattern template using tailor's tacks. Make pleats on front and back pieces **20** by bringing markers together on right side of fabric to form pleats. Press pleats towards outer edges of bag on wrong side (**A**).

Step 2
Pin front and back sections to corresponding front and back wadding sections **21** and machine-baste together (**B**). See **Using Sew-in Interfacing**, page 17.

Step 3
Transfer * marks from pattern template onto front and back pieces using tailor's tacks. Refer to **Basic Stitches**, page 12. Pin the two front/back pieces together, right sides of main fabric together.

Stitch together at side and lower edges between * marks, leaving corners free (**C**). Back-stitch at * marks as reinforcement. Fold the lower corners of the bag matching seams, and stitch straight across to form gusset.

Step 4
Make tie handles by folding each handle section **22** in half lengthways along fold line, with wrong sides together. Stitch down open sides leaving straight end open for turning.

Step 5
Pin handles to front and back sections, centring over pleats and with raw edges even. The points on the ties should face in opposite directions. Baste in place (**D**).

Step 6
Attach magnetic snap to each side of lining at position marked on pattern piece. Refer to **Magnetic Snaps**, page 24.

Step 7
Transfer * marks from pattern template onto front and back lining pieces using tailor's tacks. Pin the two front/back lining pieces together, right sides of main fabric together. Stitch together at side and lower edges between * marks, leaving corners free and leaving a gap of about 5in (13cm) for turning. Back-stitch at * marks to reinforce. Fold the lower corners of the bag matching seams, and stitch straight across in order to form a gusset.

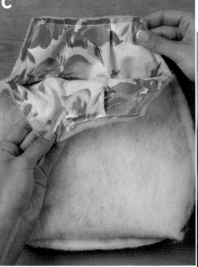

Step 8

With the bag right side out, insert it into the lining. Pin with raw edges even on each side of the bag, with * marks matched (**E**). Stitch between * marks either side of the bag, around side and upper edges (the handles will be sandwiched between). Make a few back-stitches at * marks as reinforcement. Clip corners and clip carefully into side seams at * marks.

Step 9

Turn the bag right side out through the opening. Push upper corners outwards. Insert plastic canvas into bottom of bag through opening in lining. Slip-stitch opening closed and insert lining into bag. Press top edges and bag thoroughly.

To make the matching corsage

you will need

* 36in (92cm) of grosgrain ribbon 1½in (4cm) wide

* 14in (36cm) of grosgrain ribbon 1in (2.5cm) wide for leaves

* brooch backing bar (with holes for stitching)

Step 1

Make a folded rose using the wide grosgrain ribbon. Refer to **Ribbon Roses**, page 37. Make two leaves using the narrower grosgrain ribbon, by folding and stitching as shown in picture (**F**), and hand-stitching to back of rose (**G**), covering any raw edges.

Step 2

Hand-stitch a brooch bar to the back of the corsage (**H**) and pin onto the left side of the bag front.

doris

65

1930s

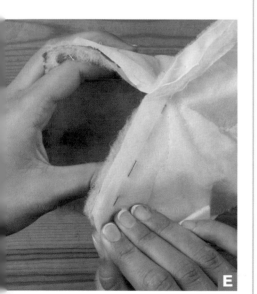

nancy

1930s RING HANDLE BAG WITH FELT FLOWER APPLIQUÉ AND MATCHING PURSE

This bag uses the same basic pattern pieces as the previous project (Doris), but has a totally different look. The shape is 1930s and the ring handle certainly has echoes of that era.

My choice of fabric is corduroy, and a lovely subtle colour like air force blue has a vintage appeal. The flowers that trim this bag are fashioned from felt, a simple craft staple, and the bag is lined with a floral cotton fabric that ties in with their colours. The flower centres are small vintage buttons, tied in with the trim on the bag flap. This deisgn also has a matching purse as the bag is big enough to house one.

dimensions

Approximately 9½in inches (24cm) deep by 10½in inches (27cm) wide (excluding handle)

pattern pieces

23 **24** **25** **26** **27**

pages 143–4

suggested fabrics

for main bag fabric:
corduroy (medium weight)

for bag lining:
floral cotton fabric

you will need

* 18in (46cm) of main fabric, 48in (122cm) wide

* 14in (36cm) of lining fabric, 36in (92cm) wide

* 14in (36cm) of wadding, 36in (92cm) wide

* one piece of fusible web 5 x 4in (13 x 10cm) for handle carrier

* one piece of iron-on interfacing 7 x 10in (18 x 26cm) for flap

* one ring handle, 5in (13cm) diameter

* three pieces of felt, 3 x 6in (8 x 15cm), in different colours for flowers

* five small buttons for trim

* four pieces of craft interfacing 1½in (4cm) square (for snap stabilizers)

* two magnetic snap sets

* one piece of plastic canvas to insert in base 8¼ x 2in (21 x 6cm)

cutting out

* Cut 2 x piece **23** (front/back) from main fabric on fold

* Cut 2 x piece **23** (front/back) from wadding on fold

* Cut 2 x piece **24** (front/back lining) from floral lining fabric on fold

* Cut 1 x piece **25** (handle carrier) from main fabric and from fusible web

* Cut 2 x piece **26** (flap) from main fabric and iron-on interfacing

* Cut 2 x piece **27** (flower template) from each of the three felt colours

making up instructions

Step 1

Make the three flower appliqués. Using the flower template ㉗, cut out two pieces in each of the three felt colours. Lay one piece on top of the other as shown in picture **A**, position on the bag front ㉓ at the bottom right (remember to account for bag seams when positioning flowers). Lay a button on top of each flower in a central position and hand-stitch in place through both of the flower pieces and the bag front (**B**).

Step 2

Attach a magnetic section of one of the snap fasteners to the bag front piece at the position marked on the pattern template. Refer to **Magnetic Snaps**, page 24.

Step 3

Pin front and back sections ㉓ to corresponding front and back wadding sections and machine-baste together. Refer to **Using Sew-in Interfacing**, page 17.

Step 4

Transfer * marks onto front and back pieces using tailor's tacks. Refer to **Basic Stitches**, page 12. Pin the two front/back pieces together, right sides of main fabric together. Stitch together at side and lower edges between * marks, leaving corners free. Back-stitch at * marks as reinforcement. Fold the lower corners of the bag matching seams, and stitch straight across to form gusset.

Step 5

Make flap. Iron interfacing onto flap pieces ㊱. Take underside flap piece only and attach non-magnetic half of the first magnetic snap, at position marked on pattern template. Place flap pieces right sides together. Stitch round side and bottom edges. Clip point and corners, then turn right side out. Press and top-stitch, ¼in (6mm) from the edge (**C**). Stitch the remaining two decorative buttons on flap near pointed end, avoiding magnetic snap.

Step 6

Make handle carrier by ironing fusible web onto reverse and folding edges marked with a dotted line on the pattern template into the centre. Refer to **Self-fabric Handles**, page 20.

Step 7

Fold handle carrier around handle, pin and stitch with raw edges even. Pin handle carrier to **front** of bag, centrally with raw edges even (). Stitch in place.

Step 8

Pin flap to **back** of bag (E), centrally with raw edges even and magnetic snap facing **outwards**. Stitch in place.

Step 9

Attach magnetic snap to each side of lining at position marked on pattern piece, using snap stabilizer.

Step 10

Transfer * marks onto front/back lining pieces using tailor's tacks. Pin the two front/back lining pieces together, right sides of main fabric together. Stitch together at side and lower edges between * marks,

leaving corners free and leaving a gap of about 6in (15cm) for turning (you must be able to get the handle through the gap). Back-stitch at * marks to reinforce. Fold the lower corners of the lining matching seams, and stitch straight across to form gusset.

Step 11

With the bag right side out, insert it into the lining. Pin with raw edges even on each side of the bag, and * marks matched. Stitch between * marks either side of the bag, round side and upper edges (the handle and flap will be sandwiched between). Make a few back-stitches at * marks as reinforcement. Clip corners and clip carefully into side seams at * marks.

Step 12

Turn the bag right side out through the opening. Push upper corners outwards. Insert plastic canvas into bottom of bag through opening in lining. Slip-stitch opening closed and turn lining into bag. Press bag thoroughly, concentrating on the top edges (F).

nancy

69

1930s

making vintage bags

To make the matching purse

you will need

* 8in (21cm) of main fabric, 20in (51cm) wide

* 8in (21cm) of iron-on interfacing, 20in (51cm) wide

* 8in (21cm) of floral lining fabric, 20in (51cm) wide

* 6in (15cm) zipper

* one piece of felt, 3 x 6in (8 x 15cm) for flower

* one piece of felt, 5 x 4in (13 x 10cm) for leaf appliqué

* one piece of fusible web, 5 x 4in (13 x 10cm) for leaf appliqué

* one small button for flower centre

cutting out

Using the main Purse template:

* Cut 2 x piece **91** (front/back) from main fabric

* Cut 2 x piece **91** (front/back) from iron-on interfacing

* Cut 2 x piece **91** (front/back) from floral lining fabric

* Cut 2 x piece **37** (flower template) from felt

* Cut 1 x each piece of the small and large leaf templates on page 144 from felt

Step 1

Iron fusible web onto the reverse of the felt for the leaves. Cut out the two leaves using the pattern templates (one each of large and small). Fuse lower leaf in place on purse front at left side, taking purse seam allowances into account. Set a narrow zigzag stitch on the machine and stitch around outside edge of leaf and down centre (see **Sewing Tip**, right).

Step 2

Position the second leaf overlapping the first, fuse and zigzag stitch in place.

Step 3

Cut two flower pieces from felt, lay one piece on top of the other as shown in the bag instructions and position on purse front overlapping leaves. Lay a button on top of the flower in a central position and hand-stitch in place through both of the flower pieces and the purse front.

Step 4

Assemble purse. Refer to **Making Matching Purses**, page 31.

Felt is a wonderful textile to use for appliqué. As the leaf appliqué for this bag is made from felt, you can use a more open zigzag stitch on the sewing machine because the raw edges will not fray, and therefore do not need to be encased as tightly.

If you use a contrasting thread for the zigzag stitch, the stitches will show and give a more homespun appearance.

nancy

71

1930s

lois

1930s BAG WITH DRAPED BUCKLE TRIM

This bag is delightfully dressy in style and features an antique metal buckle, attached with a swathe of sheer fabric. It still has the characteristic flat styling of the early 1930s clutch, but I've added a wrist strap for ease of use.

I first saw a simple and appealing bag with this silhouette in an original late 1930s mail-order catalogue and thought it would make a great shape for embellishment. For this project I've used a smart woven English silk fabric for the main body and added the shot silk drape to give the front an extra dimension. The drape is caught in the centre with a decorative buckle. Using a vintage buckle is an excellent way of combining a piece of the past in your modern handbag (see page 75 for more ideas for attractive buckles).

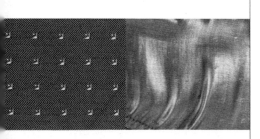

dimensions

Approximately 7½in (19cm) deep by 10½in (27cm) wide (excluding handle)

pattern pieces

28 **29** **30** page 145–6

suggested fabrics

for main bag fabric:
woven silk brocade
(firm weight)

for bag lining:
plain or patterned silk

for the swathe:
sheer fabric, with two-tone finish if possible

you will need

* 18in (46cm) of main fabric, 36in (92cm) wide
* 8in (21cm) x 16in (41cm) of sheer fabric for drape trim
* 12in (31cm) of lining fabric, 36in (92cm) wide
* 12 x 14in (31 x 36cm) of sew-in craft interfacing
* 12 x 14in (31 x 36cm) of wadding
* 12 x 14in (31 x 36cm) of iron-on interfacing
* 18in (46cm) of grosgrain ribbon for handle backing, approximately 1in (25mm) wide
* piece of fusible web 4 x 18in (10 x 46cm) for handle
* zip fastener, 7in (18cm) length
* vintage-style buckle, approximately 2in (6cm) deep

cutting out

* Cut 2 x piece **28** (front/back) from main fabric
* Cut 2 x piece **28** (front/back) from lining fabric
* Cut 1 x piece **28** (front/back) from iron-on interfacing
* Cut 1 x piece **28** (front/back) from craft interfacing
* Cut 1 x piece **28** (front/back) from wadding
* Cut 1 x piece **29** (front drape overlay) from sheer fabric on fold
* Cut 1 x piece **30** (handle) from main fabric and fusible web on fold

making up instructions

Step 1

Pin front piece ㉘ to wadding and then back with craft interfacing ㉘ piece. The wadding will be sandwiched between the fabric and the interfacing. Machine-baste all layers together around outside edge. Refer to **Using Sew-in Interfacing,** page 17.

Step 2

Machine-neaten top and bottom edges of front drape overlay ㉙ by stitching over the edges using a close and narrow zigzag stitch (**A**). This will prevent fraying. After neatening, turn over a small hem and top-stitch about ¼in (6mm) from each edge. Thread the drape through the buckle and position centrally, arranging gathers evenly (**B**).

Step 3

Pin drape in place on front between positions marked on pattern piece (**C**). Raw edges of drape should be even with side edges of bag front. Stitch in place ¼in (6mm) from the edge. From wrong side of front, hand-stitch through to right side and secure drape in place at several points along buckle (**D**).

Step 4

Iron fusible web onto reverse of handle ㉚, peel off paper backing, turn in long edges to centre and fuse in place. Stitch strip of grosgrain ribbon centrally over join. Refer to **Self-fabric Handles,** page 20. Baste the raw edges of the handle together at bottom edge, with fabric side out.

Step 5

Pin the handle to the bag front piece, centring over centre front, and machine-baste to bag over the previous row of basting (**E**).

Step 6

Iron interfacing onto back piece. Pin back piece to back lining piece, mark zip placement onto interfacing side of back and set zipper in. Refer to **How to Set in a Back Zipper,** page 28. Remember to leave the zipper **open** after setting in, as you will turn the bag through this.

Step 7

Pin the interfaced front and back sections together, right sides of main fabric together. Stitch right around entire outside edge, through main bag pieces, including handle, leaving a ½in (13mm) seam allowance. Leave the lining

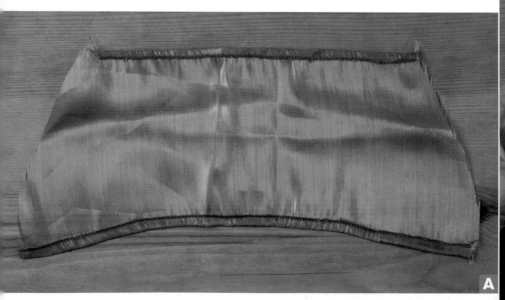

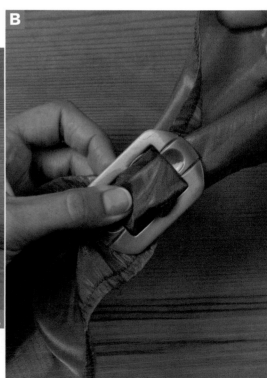

piece **free**. Clip into the seam allowance at intervals around curved edges.

Step 8

Pin the remaining lining piece to the back lining (which is now attached to the back via the zip) and stitch pieces together around entire outside edge, leaving an opening of around 5in (13cm) at centre of lower edge for turning. Refer to **Lining a Bag with a Back Zipper**, page 29.

Step 9

Turn the bag right side out, first through the opening in the bottom of the lining and then through the zipper. Push curved edges outwards. Slip-stitch the opening in lining closed. Turn the lining into the bag; do up zipper and press bag lightly.

variations

You may be lucky enough to find an interesting **buckle** on an old garment at home. If not, it's possible to stumble upon some real treasures in **thrift stores** or **remnant shops**, often for very little cost.

If you can't find a metal buckle, a **Bakelite** or **plastic** one will suffice, and as these come in very pretty colours, you could consider making this project entirely from printed **floral** cottons, making it a perfect day bag.

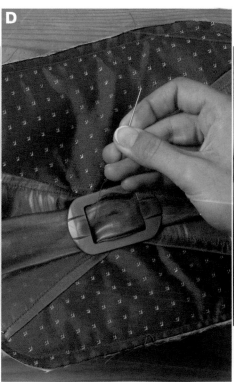

rita

1930s PLEAT BAG WITH SILK ROSE TRIM

This bag is a development of the previous project (Lois). It features pleat detailing on the front and is trimmed with a silk fabric rose and leaves, stitched at an angle. The pleats are characteristic of styles of the 1930s, but making the bag in a plain cotton twill fabric updates it for modern use.

The spotted silk trimming and light colouring of this bag give it a dressy appearance while still being summery, making it ideal for a wedding or garden party. If you don't want such a formal piece, you could always use a polka dot or candy striped cotton for the trim instead.

you will need

* 18in (46cm) of main fabric, 48in (122cm) wide

* 12in (31cm) of lining fabric, 36in (92cm) wide

* 12 x 14in (31 x 36cm) of sew-in craft interfacing

* 12 x 14in (31 x 36cm) of iron-on interfacing

* 18in (46cm) of velvet ribbon for handle trim approx 1½in (38mm) wide

* one piece of fusible web 18 x 4in (46 x 10cm) for handle

* zip fastener, 7in (18cm) length

* two squares of silk for leaves – 6 x 6in (15 x 15cm) exactly

* 22 x 4in (56 x 10cm) of polka dot silk for rose

cutting out

* Cut 1 x piece **31** (front) from main fabric on fold

* Cut 1 x piece **32** (back) from main fabric

* Cut 2 x piece **32** (back) from lining fabric

* Cut 1 x piece **32** (back) from iron-on interfacing

* Cut 1 x piece **32** (back) from sew-in craft interfacing

* Cut 1 x piece **33** (handle) from main fabric and fusible web on fold

* Cut 1 x piece **34** fabric rose from spotted silk on fold

* Cut 2 x piece **35** fabric leaf from plain silk

dimensions

Approximately 7½in (19cm) deep by 10½in (27cm) wide (excluding handle)

pattern pieces

31 **32** **33** **34** **35**

pages 146–8

suggested fabrics

for main bag fabric: medium weight cottons (twill, etc)

for bag lining: plain or quilted cotton

for the rose and leaf: polka dot and plain silk

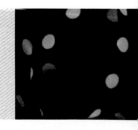

making up instructions

Step 1
Transfer makings for front pleats onto bag front, using tailor's tacks. Refer to **Basic Stitches**, page 12. Make pleats in bag front by bringing markers together on right side of fabric to form pleats. Press pleats towards outer edges of bag on wrong side (**A**). **NB: Pleats will meet in the middle on the right side of the bag and the side pleats will overlap the centre pleats on the wrong side (follow directions on pattern piece).** Baste pleats in place at top and bottom edge of bag.

Step 2
Pin front piece **31** to craft interfacing **32** piece (**B**). Machine-baste together around entire outside edge. Refer to **Using Sew-in Interfacing**, page 17.

Step 3
Iron fusible web onto reverse of handle **33**, peel off paper backing, turn in long edges to centre and

fuse in place. Stitch strip of velvet ribbon centrally over join. Refer to **Self-fabric Handles**, page 20. Baste raw edges of handle together at bottom, having velvet ribbon side out.

Step 4
Pin the handle to the bag front piece, centring over centre front, and machine-baste to bag over the previous row of basting.

Step 5
Iron interfacing onto back piece. Pin back piece to back lining piece, mark zip placement onto interfacing side of back and set zipper in. Refer to **How to Set in a Back Zipper**, page 28. Remember to leave the zipper **open** after setting in, as you will turn the bag through this.

Step 6
Pin the interfaced front and back sections together, right sides of main fabric together. Stitch front

and back together around entire outside edge, including handle, but leaving the lining piece free. Stitch with a ½in (13mm) seam allowance. Clip into the seam allowance at intervals around curved edges.

Step 9
Pin the remaining lining piece to the back lining (which is now attached to the back via the zip) and stitch pieces together around entire outside edge, leaving an opening of around 5in (13cm) at centre of lower edge for turning. Refer to **Lining a Bag with a Back Zipper**, page 29.

Step 10
Turn the bag right side out, first through the opening in the bottom of the lining and then through the zipper. Push curved edges outwards. Slip-stitch the opening in lining closed. Turn the lining into

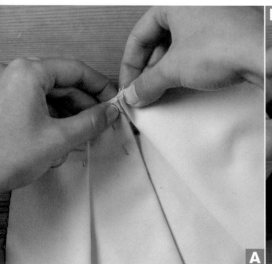

A

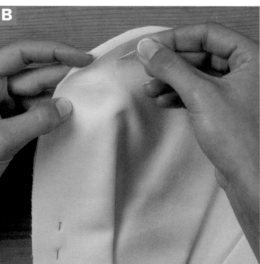

B

C

D

making **vintage** bags

the bag; do up zipper, and then press the bag using a cloth.

Step 11

Make a fabric rose from the polka dot silk. Fold the rose ㉞ piece in half lengthways and press. Machine stitch curved long raw edges together approximately ¼in (6mm) from raw edge. Run a gathering stitch along the previous row of stitches and pull gathers up (**C**). Coil into a flower shape and secure with hand-stitches at the back (**D**).

Step 12

Cut two leaf ㉟ pieces from the plain silk. Fold one square in half diagonally, then fold in half again (**E**). Stitch together along bottom raw edges, then machine neaten using a zigzag stitch. Run a gathering stitch along the previous row of stitching and pull gathers up (**F**). Fold gathers in half evenly and stitch a seam along the gathered edges (**G**).

variations

Because of the small amount of silk required to make the rose and leaf trim for this bag, and as it will be used purely decoratively, you could consider using **vintage scarves**, **hankies** or other small pieces of vintage textile. More modern **'retro' scarves** can also provide a source of interesting silk fabric – you can often pick these up in charity shops or thrift stores.

Step 13

Hand-stitch leaves together at an angle, then stitch the rose on top of the leaves. Make sure that all rough edges are covered.

Step 14

Stitch rose and leaves to bag at centre point, with leaves facing to the left at an angle.

rita

79

1930s

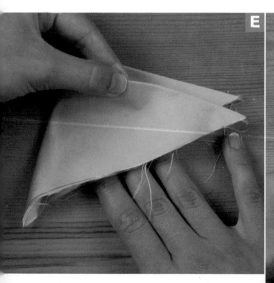

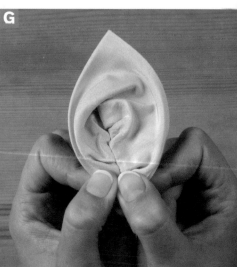

making **vintage** bags

marion

1930s SEMI-CIRCLE TWO-TONE BAG

In the mid to late 1930s, handbag shapes started to become more inventive. Although the ever-popular slimline clutch bag remained in vogue, designers began to experiment more with the actual silhouette of the bag, as well as the trim.

This bag design blends an unusual semi-circular shape, a mixture of fabrics, a pretty trim and a beaded handle. This combination produces a highly original lightweight bag, which can be used for day or evening and could be made up in endless fabric combinations. I've made this bag in contrasting tones and textures using black fake suede and lilac wool, and have trimmed it with small understated ribbon bows and roses. The handle is made from black wooden beads.

dimensions

Approximately 7½in (19cm) deep by 10½in (27cm) wide (excluding handle)

pattern pieces

pages 149–50

suggested fabrics

for main bag fabric:
fake suede or leather and wool/tweed

for bag lining:
plain silk (firm weight), or quilted lining fabric

you will need

* 12in (31cm) of main fabric, 36in (92cm) wide
* 12in (31cm) of contrast fabric, 20in (51cm) wide
* 12in (31cm) of lining fabric, 36in (92cm) wide
* 12 x 15in (31 x 38cm) of sew-in craft interfacing
* 12 x 15in (31 x 38cm) of iron-on interfacing
* 12 x 15in (31 x 38cm) of wadding
* zip fastener, 7in (18cm) length
* 14in (36cm) of wire for handle (16 gauge or 1.2mm diameter)
* approximately 26 round size 10mm wooden beads (with large holes)
* square of fusible web 4 x 5in (10 x 13cm) for handle carrier
* three small ribbon bows
* three small ribbon roses

cutting out

* Cut 1 x piece 36 (front centre panel) from main fabric
* Cut 2 x piece 37 (front side panel) from contrast fabric
* Cut 1 x piece 38 (back) from main fabric
* Cut 1 x piece 38 (back) from iron-on interfacing
* Cut 1 x piece 38 (back) from craft interfacing
* Cut 1 x piece 38 (back) from wadding
* Cut 2 x piece 38 (back) from lining fabric
* Cut 1 x piece 39 (handle carrier) from main fabric and fusible web

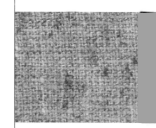

making up instructions

Step 1

Pin front centre panel piece **36** and front side panel pieces **37** together along edges marked with dotted line on pattern pieces (**A**). Baste and machine stitch together, leaving a ½in (13mm) seam allowance (**B**). Press seams toward outer edges. Pin assembled front piece to wadding **38** and then back with craft interfacing piece **38**. The wadding will be sandwiched between the fabric and the interfacing.

Step 2

Machine stitch together through all layers around the outside, approximately ¼ inch (6mm) from the edge. Then, using a long stitch length, stitch along the seams of the front panels.

Step 3

Make one handle using the wire and beads, refer to **Beaded Ring**

Handles, page 22. Iron fusible web onto reverse of handle carrier **39**, peel off paper backing, turn in edges marked with a dotted line on pattern piece to centre and fuse in place.

Step 4

Fold handle carrier around beaded ring handle (**C**) and machine-baste bottom edges together, about ½in (13mm) from raw edges.

Step 5

Pin the handle carrier to the bag front piece, centring over centre front, and machine-baste to bag over the previous row of basting (**D**).

Step 6

Iron interfacing onto back piece. Pin back piece to back lining piece, mark zip placement onto interfacing side of back and set zip

in. Refer to **How to Set in a Back Zipper**, page 28. Remember to leave the zipper **open** after setting in, as you will turn the bag through this later.

Step 7

Pin the interfaced front and back sections together, right sides of main fabric together. Stitch right around outside edge (top and curved edges), through main bag pieces, including handle carrier, leaving a ½in (13mm) seam allowance. Leave the lining piece **free** (**E**). Trim the seam allowance back to ⅜in (1cm) and clip into the seam allowance at intervals around corners and curved edge.

Step 8

Pin the remaining lining piece to the back lining (which is now attached to the back via the zipper) and stitch pieces together at the

making **vintage** bags

sides and lower edges, leaving an opening of around 5in (13cm) at centre of lower edge for turning. **NB: Gap must be large enough to get handle through.** Refer to **Lining a Bag with a Back Zipper,** page 29.

Step 9

Turn the bag right side out through the opening in the bottom of the lining and the zipper. Push corners and curved edges outwards. Slip-stitch the opening in lining closed. Turn the lining into the bag; do up the zipper, and press the bag using a cloth.

Step 10

Secure handle in place by making a few hand-stitches on either side of the handle carrier, tight up against the beads. This will stop the handle from sliding around and showing the join in the wire.

variations

If you don't want to make a beaded handle, you can always use a purchased **'ring' handle** in metal or plastic. Stick to sizes between 4 and 5in (10 and 13cm) in diameter to keep in proportion with the bag. There are many **circular handle** options available. Just remember to pick a finish – like **tortoiseshell** or **antique-effect metal** – that adds to the vintage look.

Step 11

Position ribbon bows evenly spaced down the left side of the front panel and hand-stitch in place. Finally, stitch a ribbon rose on top of each bow (**F**).

making **vintage** bags

1940s

martha

1940s FLOUNCE BAG WITH SAUSAGE DOG

This bag is one of my favourites, partly because of the pretty flounce top and partly because of the sausage dog appliqué.

In the 1940s and 50s, accessories were often trimmed with whimsical appliqués and dogs, particularly poodles, featured high on the list. I found a picture of a dachshund in an original 1940s home sewing pattern and felt that a variation would make a witty trim for my flounce bag. This velvet appliqué is a refreshing alternative to the plastic print images often found on modern bags. Made from serviceable wool tweed, it is given a touch of glamour with the velvet flounce.

dimensions

Approximately 8in (21cm) deep by 11½in (29cm) wide (excluding handle)

pattern pieces

40 41 42 43 44

pages 151–2

suggested fabrics

for main bag fabric:
wool or tweed fabrics

for the flounce and appliqué:
cotton velvet fabric

for bag lining:
quilted lining fabric

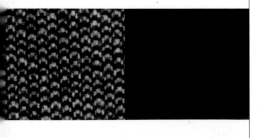

you will need

* 20in (51cm) of main fabric, 48in (122cm) wide

* 22in (56cm) of iron-on interfacing, 36in (92cm) wide

* 14in (36cm) of quilted lining fabric, 36in (92cm) wide

* 14in (36cm) of velvet for flounce, 36in (92cm) wide

* piece of velvet or felt 6 x 8in (15 x 21cm) for dog appliqué

* piece of fusible web 6 x 8in (16 x 21cm) for dog appliqué

* piece of narrow ribbon approximately 8in (21cm) long for dog's collar and bow

* one 4mm bead and one tiny seed bead for dog's eye

* two pieces x 1½in (4cm) square of craft interfacing (for snap stabilizers)

* one magnetic snap set

* piece of plastic canvas 9¾ x 3in (25 x 8cm) to insert in base

cutting out

* Cut 2 x piece **40** (front/back) from main fabric

* Cut 2 x piece **40** (front/back) from iron-on interfacing

* Cut 2 x piece **40** (front/back) from quilted lining fabric

* Cut 2 x piece **41** (handle) from main fabric on fold

* Cut 1 x piece **41** (handle) from iron-on interfacing on fold

* Cut 4 x piece **42** (flounce) from velvet

* Cut 1 x sausage dog appliqué **43** from velvet (or felt) and 1 from fusible web

* Cut 2 x dog's ear **44** from velvet (1 in reverse), and 1 from fusible web

making up instructions

Step 1

Iron interfacing onto reverse of front and back **40** sections. Ensure that you follow the manufacturer's guidelines.

Step 2

Make dog appliqué. Iron fusible web onto reverse of velvet (or felt) for appliqué, cut out sausage dog template **43**, draw onto paper side of web and cut out (remember to draw dog in reverse). Fuse in place on bag front (at lower right side) then satin stitch round outside edge of appliqué. Refer to **How to Add a Flat Appliqué**, page 34. Fuse the two ear pieces **44** together, satin stitch around the outside of the ear, then stitch the ear to the dog around the upper curved edge only.

Step 3

Pin the two front/back pieces right sides of main fabric together.

Stitch together at side and lower edges, leaving corners free. Fold the lower corners of the bag matching seams, and stitch straight across to form gusset.

Step 4

Make flounce. Stitch two flounce **42** pieces together at sides (**A**). Repeat with the other two pieces. Then pin the two joined sections, right sides together, around lower curved edge (**B**). Stitch using a ½in (13mm) seam allowance. Trim seam allowance back to ⅜in (1cm), clip into seam allowance at intervals round curve, then turn flounce right sides out. Top-stitch curve neatly about ½in (13mm) from lower edge. Baste upper edges of curve together.

Step 5

Pin flounce to upper edge of bag. Match side seams with upper raw edges even (**C**). Baste in place.

Step 6

Make handle. Iron interfacing onto reverse side of both handle **41** pieces. Pin handles right sides together and stitch down both long edges leaving a ½in (13mm) seam allowance. Clip curves and then turn handle right sides out. Press and top-stitch down both sides.

Step 7

Pin handle to bag centrally at front and back, raw edges even, and stitch in place (**D**). You will be stitching through the flounce also.

Step 8

Attach a magnetic snap to each side of lining at position marked on pattern piece. Refer to **Magnetic Snaps**, page 24.

Step 9

Pin the two front/back lining pieces together, right sides of main fabric together. Stitch together at

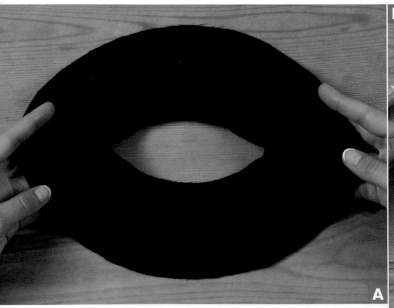

making **vintage** bags

side and lower edges leaving a gap of about 5in (13cm) for turning, and leaving corners free. Fold the lower corners of the lining matching seams, and stitch straight across to form gusset.

Step 10

With the bag right side out, insert it into the lining. Pin with raw edges even and side seams matched. Stitch bag and lining together around upper edge (the handle and flounce will be sandwiched between). Trim seam allowance back to ⅜in (1cm) and clip carefully into seam allowance near side seams.

Step 11

Turn the bag right side out through the opening. Roll the lining with your fingers so that it is not visible from the outside. The flounce will be facing upwards at this stage. Pin and hand-baste lining in place

around upper edge of bag (**E**). Top-stitch around the upper edge through bag and lining, about ¾in (18mm) from the top of the bag, using a medium to long stitch length and taking extra care when sewing through the bulkier areas.

Step 12

Insert plastic canvas into bottom of bag through the opening in the lining. Slip-stitch the opening closed and insert lining into bag. Turn flounce downwards and press bag thoroughly (do not press flounce – the velvet will mark).

Step 13

Make a small bow by cutting a short piece of ribbon that is the length of the dog's neck plus a ¼in (6mm) each end to fold under. Hand-stitch ribbon to the dog's neck along the top and bottom edges of ribbon, then stitch bow over collar.

Step 14

Stitch a bead on for the dog's eye. Thread a fine needle with a double length of thread and tie a knot at the end. Take the needle up through the appliqué where you want the eye to be, thread on the 4mm bead and the seed bead. Skip the seed bead then take the needle back through the 4mm bead only. Secure with a few stitches at the back of the appliqué. For extra security, you can go through the beads a second time.

making **vintage** bags

To make the matching purse

you will need

* 8in (21cm) of main fabric, 20in (51cm) wide

* 8in (21cm) of iron-on interfacing, 20in (51cm) wide

* 8in (21cm) of quilted lining fabric, 20in (51cm) wide

* 6in (15cm) zipper

* Piece of velvet 6 x 8in (15 x 21cm) for dog appliqué

* Piece of fusible web 6 x 8in (15 x 21cm) for dog appliqué

* Piece of narrow lace (or ribbon) approximately 3in (8cm) long for dog's collar

* Small ribbon rose for dog's collar

* Bead for dog's eye – 1 x 4mm bead and 1 tiny seed bead

cutting out

Using the main purse template:

* Cut 2 x piece **91** (front/back) from main fabric

* Cut 2 x piece **91** (front/back) from iron-on interfacing

* Cut 2 x piece **91** (front/back) from floral lining fabric

I have given the dog a ribbon and bow collar on the bag (detail shown, right), and have used glass beads for the eye. I've varied the matching purse very slightly by using a piece of antique lace and a ribbon rose as a variation on the collar (detail shown, far right).

Step 1

Cut out and apply dog appliqué following instructions as for main bag. Refer also to **Flat Appliqué**, page 34. Place the appliqué on the right side of the purse piece where you want it to be, and then fuse the appliqué into place using an iron and following the manufacturer's instructions (**A**).

Step 2

Machine stitch the appliqué shape all around the outside edge using a 'satin stitch' (**B**).

Step 3

Make the ear for the dog and machine stitch it in place around the top only so that it retains a three-dimensional feel (**C**).

Step 4

Cut a short piece of lace the length of the dog's neck plus a ¼in (6mm) each end to fold under. Hand-stitch neatly in place along top and bottom edges of lace, then stitch rose onto collar. Stitch a bead on for the eye.

Step 5

Assemble purse referring to **Making Matching Purses**, page 31.

martha

91

1940s

veronica

1940s TAPESTRY BAG WITH BUTTERFLY TRIM AND MATCHING PURSE

This bag is actually based on a style from 1943 with a short handle attached with d-rings. I have modernized it by adding a slightly longer strap which enables the bag to be carried on the shoulder and tucked under the arm.

In the 1940s larger and more functional bags started to appear. This bag would be suitable for day wear. It is made in a carefully chosen tapestry fabric of 'antique' colours, trimmed with a velvet ribbon and a pretty leather butterfly.

you will need

* 20in (51cm) of main fabric, minimum 36in (92cm) wide

* 18in (46cm) of lining fabric, 36in (92cm) wide

* 18in (46cm) of firm weight iron-on interfacing, 36in (92cm) wide

* 40in (102cm) of velvet ribbon, 1in (25mm) wide for handle and front trim

* piece of fusible web 26 x 3in (66 x 8cm) for handle

* 8 x 4in (21 x 10cm) of soft leather for butterfly

* 8 x 4in (21 x 10cm) of felt (to back leather)

* 8 x 4in (21 x 10cm) of fusible web

* bead, button or beaded trim for butterfly centre

* two pieces of craft interfacing 1½in (4cm) square (for snap stabilizers)

* one magnetic snap set

* piece of plastic canvas to insert in base 12 x 1¼in (31 x 3cm)

cutting out

* Cut 2 x piece **45** (front/back) from main fabric

* Cut 2 x piece **45** (front/back) from iron-on interfacing

* Cut 2 x piece **45** (front/back) from quilted lining fabric

* Cut 1 x piece **46** (single fold handle) from main fabric on fold

* Cut 1 x piece **46** (single fold handle) from fusible web on fold

* Cut 1 x large butterfly piece **47** from each of leather, felt and fusible web

* Cut 1 x small butterfly piece **48** from each of leather, felt and fusible web

* Cut ribbon into lengths of 12in (31cm) for front trim and 23in (59cm) for handle

dimensions

Approximately 8in (20cm) deep by 14in (36cm) wide (excluding handle)

pattern pieces

45 **46** **47** **48**

pages 153–4

suggested fabrics

for main bag fabric:
tapestry or brocade fabrics

for bag lining:
quilted lining fabric

Step 1

Iron interfacing onto front and back sections **45** following the manufacturer's guidelines.

Step 2

Pin the 12in (31cm) strip of velvet ribbon onto the front piece **45** in position marked on pattern piece (**A**). Machine stitch in place along both edges of ribbon. Press lightly through a cloth from the back.

Step 3

Pin the two interfaced front/back pieces right sides of main fabric together. Stitch round sides and lower edges, leaving a ½in (13mm) seam allowance. Insert your finger into each one of the bottom corners. Match up seam on the bottom and side, pin through all thicknesses and stitch straight across the corner to form a gusset. Clip the seam allowance at the corner (**B**).

Step 4

Repeat this on the opposite corner. Turn bag right sides out and press.

Step 5

Make handle by ironing fusible web onto reverse side of handle piece and folding long edges in to centre. Fuse in place, then pin ribbon centrally onto handle, covering join (**C**). Machine stitch in place along both edges of ribbon. Refer to **Self-fabric Handles**, page 20.

Step 6

On outside, position centred over side seams with raw edges even, pin handle to bag (ribbon side against bag) and baste it in place.

Step 7

On lining pieces, transfer snap marker positions and fix magnetic snaps using stabilizer interfacing squares. Refer to **Magnetic Snaps**, page 24.

Step 8

Stitch lining pieces together at sides and lower edges, leaving an opening of around 5in (13cm) at the centre of the lower edge for turning. Insert your finger into one of the bottom corners. Match up seam on bottom and side, pin through all thicknesses and stitch straight across the corner to form a gusset as you did for the main bag pieces. Clip seam allowance at corner. Repeat this on the opposite corner.

Step 9

Insert bag into lining with right sides together. Pin lining to bag and baste together around upper edges. Pin and baste through all thicknesses, including handles. Machine stitch through all thicknesses using a medium stitch length and leaving a seam allowance of ½in (13mm). Stitch slowly and carefully, especially over the handle. Trim the seam back to around ⅜in (1cm) to

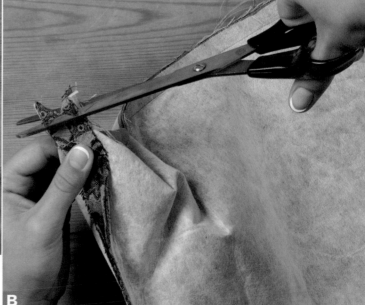

eliminate bulk. Clip into seam
allowance around curve.

Step 10

Turn the bag right side out through
the opening in the bottom of the
lining. Insert plastic canvas
rectangle into base and then
slip-stitch the opening closed. Turn
the lining into the bag. Refer to
How to Line a Top-opening Bag,
page 26.

Step 11

Roll the lining with your fingers so
that it is not visible from the
outside, pin and hand-baste it in
place around upper edge of bag.
Top-stitch through all layers, about
¾in (18mm) from the top of the
bag, using a medium to long stitch
length and taking extra care when
sewing through the bulkier areas.
Do up the snap and then give the
bag a press.

Step 12

Make the leather butterfly. Cut out
one each of large and small
butterfly pattern pieces from
leather, fusible web and felt. Iron
fusible web onto reverse of felt,
peel off paper backing then fuse
leather pieces to felt pieces,
through a cloth and from the felt
side. Machine stitch around
outside edge of each butterfly,
around ¼in (6mm) from the edge.
Lay small butterfly on top of large
butterfly and stitch together down
the centre.

Step 13

Make a beaded centre trim, or use
a decorative button or long bead.
Stitch this to butterfly using a
sharp needle (**D**). Stitch butterfly
to bag positioned over the ribbon
trim, at an angle and to one side of
the bag.

variations

I have made a beaded
centre for the butterfly
on this bag, but it
would look equally
good with one or two
long beads or a
decorative **button** as
a midpoint. Whatever
you choose will help to
create the vintage look
of the bag.

veronica

95

1940s

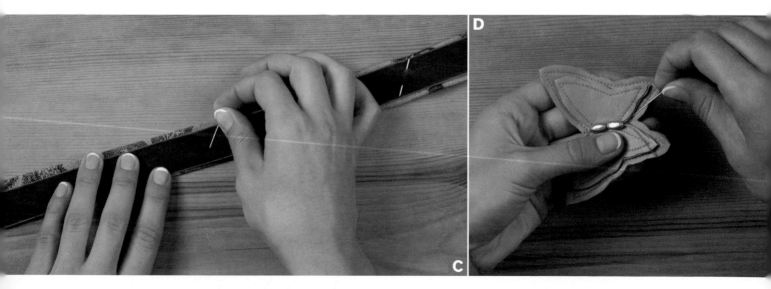

To make the matching purse

you will need

* 8in (21cm) of main fabric, 20in (51cm) wide

* 8in (21cm) of iron-on interfacing, 20in (51cm) wide

* 8in (21cm) of lining fabric, 20in (51cm) wide

* 6in (15cm) zipper

* 8in (21cm) of velvet ribbon, 1in (25mm) wide for front trim

* 7 x 4in (18 x 10cm) of leather for butterfly

* 7 x 4in (18 x 10cm) of felt (to back leather)

* 7 x 4in (18 x 10cm) of fusible web

* Bead, button or beaded trim for butterfly centre

cutting out

Using the purse template:

* Cut 2 x piece **91** (front/back) from main fabric

* Cut 2 x piece **91** (front/back) from iron-on interfacing

* Cut 2 x piece **91** (front/back) from lining fabric

* Cut 1 x tiny butterfly piece from each of leather, felt and fusible web

* Cut 1 x small butterfly piece **48** from each of leather, felt and fusible web

Step 1

Pin the strip of velvet ribbon onto the front piece **91**, with the top edge of the ribbon approximately 1¾in (45mm) from the top of the front piece. Machine stitch in place along both edges of ribbon, then press lightly through a cloth from the reverse.

Step 2

Make leather butterfly. Cut out one each of tiny and small butterfly pattern pieces from leather, fusible web and felt. Iron fusible web onto reverse of felt, peel off paper backing then fuse leather pieces to felt pieces, through a cloth and from the felt side. Complete butterfly trim following instructions for main bag.

Step 3

Assemble purse referring to section on **Making Matching Purses**, page 31.

Step 4

Hand-stitch butterfly in place on purse front. Butterfly should be stitched over the ribbon, at an angle and to the left side of the purse.

When sewing leather on a domestic sewing machine, it is advisable to use a special foot. If you use a regular machine foot, the leather can stick to the foot and cause dragging. Using a Teflon foot or a roller foot will help to stop this. Also, having the felt on the reverse of the butterfly appliqué will prevent sticking or damage to the leather from the underside. It will then be easier to hand-stitch the butterfly to the bag via the felt backing instead of having to stitch through the leather.

veronica

97

1940s

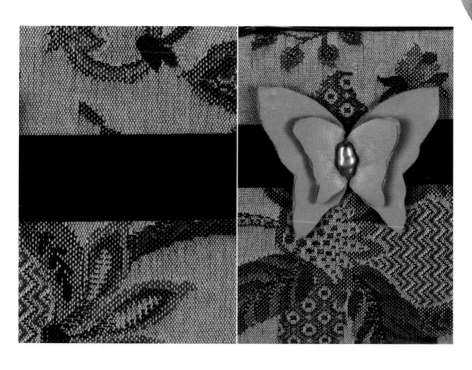

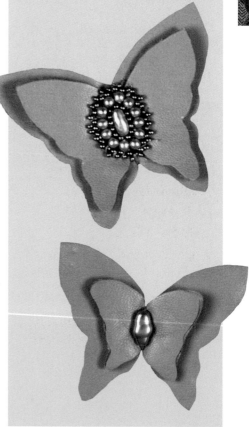

grace

1940s WOOL LEAF APPLIQUÉ BAG

This bag has been made in a plain tone wool fabric with a matching felt leaf appliqué. This, along with the decorative braid edging and frog fastener, gives an almost oriental feel to the bag, which really suits the simplicity of the design.

This is a fairly simple bag to construct and has no facings, instead having a quilted lining. It is a very good basic style to use as a blank canvas for embellishment. It fastens with a touch and close magnetic snap – the frog fastener is decorative. The bag benefits from inserting a strip of plastic canvas into the bottom to give some structure.

dimensions

Approximately 8in (21cm) deep by 14in (36cm) wide (excluding handle)

pattern pieces

49 **50** **51** **52**

pages 155–6

suggested fabrics

for main bag fabric:
firm plain wool fabrics

for bag lining:
quilted lining fabric

you will need

✳ 20in (51cm) of main fabric, minimum 36in (92cm) wide

✳ 18in (46cm) of quilted lining fabric, 36in (92cm) wide

✳ If making a pocket, you will also need a rectangle of lining 5½ x 8½in (14 x 22cm)

✳ 18in (46cm) of craft weight sew-in interfacing, 36in (92cm) wide

✳ 9 x 6in (23 x 15cm) of black felt for main leaf appliqué

✳ 9 x 6in (23 x 15cm) of beige felt

✳ five small vintage buttons

✳ 25in (64cm) of black gimp braid

✳ one decorative frog fastener

✳ two pieces of square craft interfacing (for snap stabilizers) 1½in (4cm)

✳ one magnetic snap set

✳ piece of plastic canvas to insert in base 12 x 1¼in (31 x 3cm)

✳ piece of fusible web for handle 26 x 4in (66 x 10cm)

cutting out

✳ Cut 2 x piece **49** (front/back) from main fabric

✳ Cut 2 x piece **49** (front/back) from craft interfacing

✳ Cut 2 x piece **49** (front/back) from quilted lining fabric

✳ Cut 1 x piece **50** (double fold handle) from main fabric on fold

✳ Cut 1 x piece **50** (double fold handle) from fusible web on fold

✳ Cut 1 x piece **51** (main leaf appliqué) from black felt and fusible web

✳ Cut 1 x piece **52** (leaf overlay appliqué) from beige felt and fusible web

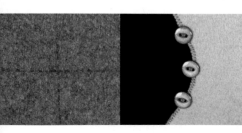

making up instructions

Step 1
Pin front and back sections **49** to corresponding front and back interfacing sections **49** and baste-stitch together. Refer to **Using Sew-in Interfacing**, page 17.

Step 2
Iron fusible web onto reverse of appliqué pieces and peel off paper backing. Position main leaf piece on lower left of bag front (allowing for bag seam allowance) and fuse in place. Position overlay leaf piece on top of main leaf, as shown in picture (**A**), and fuse in place. Satin stitch pieces round all raw edges, then stitch buttons along curve as shown. Refer to **Flat Appliqué**, page 34.

Step 3
Pin the two interfaced front/back pieces together, right sides of main fabric together. Stitch round sides and lower edges, leaving a 1/2in (13mm) seam allowance. Insert your finger into each one of the bottom corners. Match up seam on

bottom and side, pin through all thicknesses and stitch straight across the corner to form a gusset. Clip seam allowance at corner.

Step 4
Repeat this on the opposite corner. Turn bag right sides out and press.

Step 5
Make handle by ironing fusible web onto reverse side of handle piece, folding in long edges to centre, then folding in half lengthways again and top-stitching together down open side. Refer to section on **Self-fabric Handles**, page 20.

Step 6
Pin handle to outside of bag, centred over side seams with raw edges even. Baste in place (**B**).

Step 7
On lining pieces **49**, transfer snap marker positions and fix magnetic snaps using stabilizer interfacing squares. Refer to **Magnetic Snaps**, page 24.

Step 8
Optional: make pocket. Cut a rectangle of lining fabric measuring 5½ x 8½in (14 x 22cm). Fold it in half, right sides together. Stitch up each side leaving the bottom open. Clip the corners and turn right sides out (**C**). Stitch the lower edges of the pocket together, clip corners and machine-neaten (use a fairly close zigzag stitch).

Step 9
Attach pocket to back lining by placing it with the outside of the pocket against the right side of the lining, with the neatened edge upwards (**D**). Stitch pocket to lining along bottom edge. Turn pocket upwards and stitch to lining at side edges, approximately 1/4in (6mm) from the edges.

Step 10
Stitch lining pieces together at sides and lower edges, leaving an opening of around 5in (13cm) at centre of lower edge for turning. Insert your finger into one of the

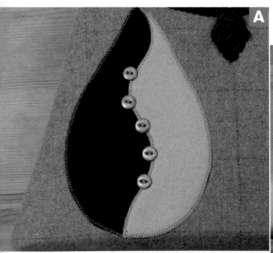

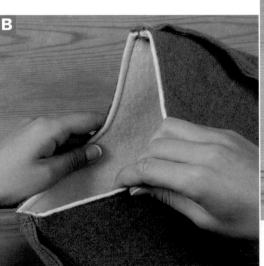

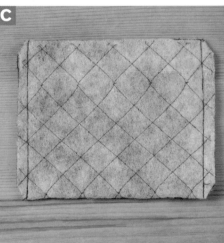

bottom corners. Match up seam on bottom and side, pin through all thicknesses and stitch straight across the corner to form a gusset as you did for the main bag pieces. Clip seam allowance at corners. Repeat this on the opposite corner.

Step 11

Insert bag into lining, with right sides together. Pin lining to bag with raw edges even and baste together around upper edges (**E**). Pin and baste through all thicknesses, including handles. Machine stitch through all thicknesses using a medium stitch length and leaving a seam allowance of ½in (13mm). Stitch slowly and carefully, especially over the handle. Trim the seam back to around ⅜in (1cm) to eliminate bulk. Clip into seam allowance at curve.

Step 12

Turn the bag right side out through the opening in the bottom of the lining. Insert plastic canvas rectangle into base, and then slip-stitch the opening closed.

variations

I have included **an internal pocket** in this bag, just large enough to house a small mirror. You can omit the pocket if you wish – likewise if you want to, you can use this method of pocket construction to add a pocket to any of the bags in the book. Pockets work well with this bag because it is quite large and there is plenty of room on the lining for it.

Internal pockets were a strong feature of vintage bags, and many shop-bought varieties actually included a **mirror** with the bag. Apart from being practical, you could use the pocket as an internal feature, perhaps making it from **contrasting** patterned fabric.

Turn the lining into the bag. Refer to **How to Line a Top-opening Bag**, page 26.

Step 13

Roll the lining with your fingers so that it is not visible from the outside, pin and hand-baste it in place around upper edge of bag. Top stitch through all layers, about ¾in (18mm) from the top of the bag, using a medium to long stitch length and taking extra care when sewing through the bulkier areas. Do up snaps and press the bag.

Step 14

Starting at one side seam, pin the gimp braid around the top of the bag, about ¼in (6mm) from the top edge. Tuck raw end of braid under to neaten. Machine stitch in place, down the centre of the braid and through all layers of the bag (fabric and lining). Tidy ends with a few hand-stitches if necessary.

Step 15

Hand-stitch a decorative frog fastener in place in a central position near the top edge (**F**).

grace

101

1940s

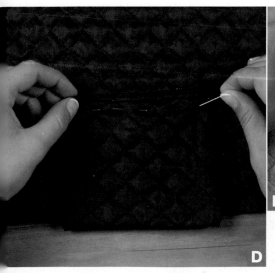

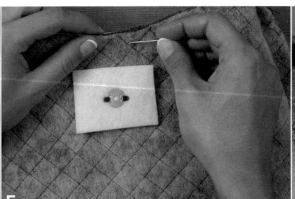

making **vintage** bags

patricia

1940s AUTUMN BOW CRESCENT BAG

This inventive crescent shape recurs quite frequently in home sewing pattern catalogues throughout the 1940s. I've seen it with various methods of fastening, but through experimenting have found that using a handle which threads through a loop at the other end is by far the most convenient for modern use.

Although it looks small and neat when done up, this is actually quite a roomy little bag. It uses wadding as a means of bulking without stiffening, which is essential as this bag relies on being soft enough to fold into its wonderful 'croissant' shape. Made in this hard-wearing wool tweed, I felt the bag could benefit from a contrasting 'statement' trim, and that's why I decided on this soft foppish velvet bow. The colour choice has also added to the period feel of this piece.

dimensions

Approximately 7in (18cm) deep by 11in (28cm) wide, when opened out

pattern pieces

53 **54** **55** **56** **57**

pages 157–8

suggested fabrics

for main bag fabric:
wool tweed or flannel
(firm weight)

for bag lining:
plain/patterned silk,
cotton prints

for the bow:
soft drapey velvet

you will need

* 17in (44cm) of main fabric, minimum 36in (92cm) wide
* 12in (31cm) x 36in (92cm) of lining fabric
* 12in (31cm) x 36in (92cm) of wadding
* 9 x 30in (23 x 77cm) of velvet for bow
* one piece of fusible web 3 x 6in (8 x 15cm) for bow centre and loop fastener
* zip fastener, 7in (18cm) length
* 17 x 10in (44 x 26cm) of iron-on interfacing for handle stiffener

cutting out

* Cut 2 x piece **53** (front/back) from main fabric
* Cut 2 x piece **53** (front/back) from lining fabric
* Cut 2 x piece **53** (front/back) from wadding
* Cut 2 x piece **54** (handle) from main fabric and iron-on interfacing
* Cut 1 x piece **55** (loop fastener) from main fabric and fusible web
* Cut 2 x piece **56** (main bow piece) from velvet
* Cut 1 x piece **57** (bow centre) from velvet and fusible web

making up instructions

Step 1

Pin front and back pieces **53** to corresponding wadding pieces. Baste together around outside edge. Refer to **Using Sew-in Interfacing**, page 17.

Step 2

Transfer * marks from pattern template using tailor's tacks. Stitch front and back sections together at upper edges, leaving open between *. Baste the section between the * marks, and press the seam open flat.

Step 3

Set in zipper referring to, **How to Set in a Top Zipper**, page 30.

Step 4

Pin and stitch front and back **53** sections together around curved edge (leaving upper corners free).

Step 5

Make handle. Iron interfacing onto the reverse of both handle pieces **54**. Pin handle pieces right sides together and stitch down each long edge, leaving short ends open (**A**). Clip curved seam allowance and turn handle right side out. Press and top-stitch about ½in (13mm) from each long edge. Baste ends together flat (**B**).

Step 6

Make loop fastener by ironing fusible web to reverse of piece **55**, folding long edges to centre and fusing in place. Fold in half lengthways again and stitch open long edges together, approximately ¼in (6mm) from the edge. Refer to, **Self-fabric Handles**, page 20.

Step 7

On outside, at one end, pin and baste handle to upper side (corner) edges of front and back, centring over seam. At other end, pin and baste loop fastener (ends of loop should be 1in (25mm) apart) (**C**).

Step 8

From the **inside**, fold the upper corners, matching seams and stitch straight across, through handle/loop fastener (**D**).

Step 9

Make lining. Stitch front and back lining sections together at upper edges, leaving open between *. Press open the seam allowance for 'open' section. Stitch front and back right sides together around curved edge, leaving upper corners free. From the **inside**, fold the upper corners, matching seams and stitch straight across.

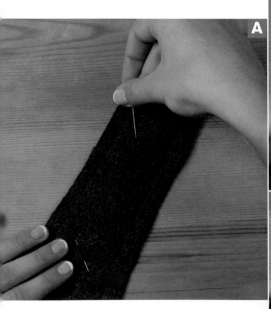

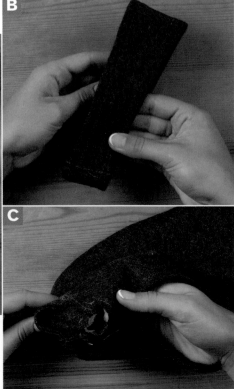

making **vintage** bags

Step 10

Turn bag inside out and insert into lining, wrong sides together. Pin the pressed edge of the lining to the zipper tape and hand slip-stitch in place (**E**).

Step 11

Construct the bow referring to **Making a Bow (Style 1: Angled Bow)**, page 35.

Step 12

Hand-stitch bow in place at loop end of bag, centring over side seam (**F**).

For many of the projects in this book, I have used short pile velveteen rather than high pile velvet. In this case I have used viscose velvet which has a lovely sheen and a deep pile – this gives it a more sumptuous look. This type of velvet can be problematic to stitch with larger items, but for small pieces like bows, it is ideal. Take care when pressing velvet of this kind – it is easy to squash the pile. Pressing lightly on top of another piece of velvet (right sides together) will help prevent the pile being flattened. However, experimenting with flattening the pile a little, particularly randomly, can result in a more vintage look.

rose

1940s NAUTICAL ROSE CRESCENT BAG

This fine-looking stripy version of the 1940s crescent bag has a nautical feel, and the dashing blue and white stripes make it ideal for toning with plain summer casuals.

This bag is made following the same method as the previous bag (Patricia, page 102) but with a few trimming changes – a bias binding trim on the handle, and a co-ordinating folded rose. Instead of using wadding as a backing for the fabric, I've given the fabric a slightly more crisp handle by using a medium iron-on interfacing on the fabric, and simply adding a quilted lining to give padding to the shape. This bag is made from striped cotton drill fabric which gives it a more hard-wearing quality. It could also be made in striped regency style silk for a more sumptuous look and feel.

dimensions

Approximately 7in (18cm) deep by 11in (28cm) wide, when opened out

pattern pieces

58 **59** **60** pages 157–8

suggested fabrics

for main bag fabric:
striped medium weight cotton drill/twill fabrics

for bag lining:
quilted lining

for the rose:
plain lightweight cotton drill/twill

you will need

* 17in (44cm) of main fabric, minimum 36in (92cm) wide

* 12 x 36in (31 x 92cm) of quilted lining fabric

* 12 x 36in (31 x 92cm) of medium weight iron-on interfacing

* one strip of plain fabric for rose, 2in (5cm) wide by approximately 30in (77cm) length (this can be cut across the width of the fabric)

* one piece of iron-on interfacing 17 x 10in (44 x 26cm) for handle stiffener

* zip fastener, 7in (18cm) length

* 98in (2.5 metres) bias binding, 1in (25mm) wide for binding handle and rose

cutting out

* Cut 2 x piece **58** (front/back) from main fabric

* Cut 2 x piece **58** (front/back) from quilted lining fabric

* Cut 2 x piece **58** (front/back) from medium weight iron-on interfacing

* Cut 2 x piece **59** (handle) from main fabric and iron-on interfacing

* Cut 1 x piece **60** (loop fastener) from main fabric and fusible web

* Cut rose strip from plain drill, 2 x 30in (5 x 77cm)

making up instructions

Step 1
Iron medium weight interfacing onto reverse side of front and back pieces **58** following manufacturer's guidelines.

Step 2
Transfer * marks from pattern template using tailor's tacks. Stitch front and back **58** sections together at upper edges, leaving open between *. Baste the section between the *, and press the seam open flat.

Step 3
Set in zipper referring to **How to Set in a Top Zipper**, page 30.

Step 4
Pin and stitch front and back **58** sections together round curved edge, leaving upper corners free.

Step 5
Make handle. Iron interfacing onto reverse side of both handle pieces **59**. Then place pieces **wrong** sides together and baste-stitch together down each long edge, about ½in (13mm) away from raw edges. Trim seam allowance to about ¼in (6mm) away from basting (**A**).

Step 6
Bind edges of handle. Stitch bias binding tape down each long edge of the handle from one side (**B**). Fold other edge of tape over raw edge and top-stitch from the other side of the handle (**C**).

Step 7
Make loop fastener by ironing fusible web onto reverse of piece **60**, bringing long edges to centre and fusing in place. Fold in half lengthways again and stitch open long edges together, approximately ¼in (6mm) from the edge. Refer to **Self-fabric Handles**, page 20.

Step 8
On the outside, at one end, pin and baste handle to upper side (corner) edges of front and back, centring over seam. At other end, pin and baste loop fastener. Refer to **Patricia**, page 102 for more details on this.

Step 9
From the **inside**, fold the upper corners, matching seams and stitch straight across, through handle/loop fastener.

Step 10
Make lining. Stitch front and back lining sections together at upper edges, leaving open between *. Press open the seam allowance for 'open' section. Stitch front and back lining right sides together around curved edge, leaving upper corners free. From the inside, fold the upper corners, matching seams and stitch straight across.

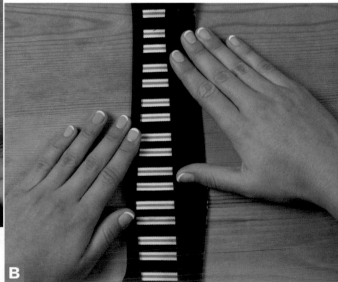

Step 11

Turn bag inside out and insert into lining, wrong sides together. Pin the pressed edge of the lining to the zipper tape and hand slip-stitch in place (see **Patricia**, page 102).

Step 12

Make the rose. Stitch bias binding tape down each long edge of rose strip as you did with the handle. Then construct a rose referring to **Ribbon Roses**, page 37 (**D**).

Step 13

Hand-stitch rose in place at loop end of bag, centring over side seam (**E**).

sewing tip

A strip of fabric edged with bias binding makes an ideal alternative to ribbon when making folded roses. Although ribbons come ready-made, we often have strips of fabric left over from a project which would make attractive roses. Fabric with both sides the same is ideal. However if you are using a fine weight patterned or floral fabric, you can stitch two strips wrong sides together down the long edges and then bind the raw edges with bias tape.

rose

109

1940s

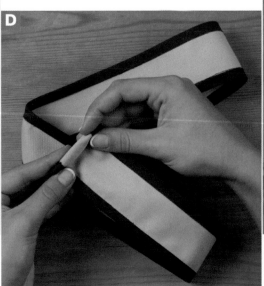

making **vintage** bags

1950s

audrey

1950s GATHERED BAG WITH FELT CORSAGE

The influence for this bag came from an antique shop find. Although the original 1950s bag had no gathered detail, no trim and a metal handle, I loved the squared shape of it.

The original bag was made from a grosgrain fabric – I've chosen a beautiful vintage-toned grey corded velvet, which is offset perfectly by the burgundy felt flower trim. The addition of a decorative felt handle gives this bag a personality all of its own.

Corsages, a fashion favourite throughout the 1930s to 50s, have made a dramatic comeback in recent years and have regularly adorned the catwalks. This felt bloom with its pearly grey leaves and simple bead centre can be detached from the bag and worn on the lapel of a smart wool jacket or a chunky jumper to add a touch of vintage chic. It makes a charming alternative to the elaborate silk corsages currently offered in fashion stores.

dimensions

Approximately 9½in (24cm) deep by 9½in (24cm) wide (excluding handle)

pattern pieces

61 62 63 64 65 66
67 68 69 70

pages 159–61

suggested fabrics

for main bag fabric:
corded velvet or similar

for bag lining:
plain or patterned lining in a toning shade

113

you will need

* 18in (46cm) of main fabric, 36in (92cm) wide
* 14 x 36in (36 x 92cm) of lining fabric
* 14 x 14in (36 x 36cm) of sew-in craft interfacing
* 14 x 14in (36 x 36cm) of iron-on interfacing
* zip fastener, 7in (18cm) length
* 5 x 18in (13 x 46cm) of felt for handle
* 4 x 8in (10 x 21cm) of plastic canvas for handle
* 4 x 16in (10 x 41cm) of craft interfacing for handle

cutting out

* Cut 1 x piece 61 (front top panel) from main fabric
* Cut 1 x piece 62 (front bottom panel) from main fabric
* Cut 1 x piece 63 (back) from main fabric
* Cut 1 x piece 63 (back) from iron-on interfacing
* Cut 1 x piece 63 (back) from craft interfacing
* Cut 2 x piece 63 (back) from lining fabric
* Cut 2 x piece 64 (handle) from felt
* Cut 2 x piece 65 (handle centre) from craft interfacing
* Cut 1 x piece 65 (handle centre) from plastic canvas

making up instructions

Step 1

Transfer * marks from front bottom pattern template **62** using tailor's tacks. Run a gathering stitch along the top (curved) edge of front bottom panel between * marks and pull gathers up to 4in (10cm) (**A**). Pin lower edge of front top panel **61** to upper edge of gathered front bottom panel piece **62**, right sides together (**B**). Baste and machine stitch together, leaving a ½in (13mm) seam allowance. Press seams toward top. Pin assembled front piece to craft interfacing **63** piece and baste-stitch together (**C**). Refer to **Using Sew-in Interfacing**, page 17.

Step 2

Make handle. Pin felt handle pieces together **right sides out**. Stitch around side and top edges only, ¼in (6mm) from the edge. Place one piece **65** of craft interfacing either side of the plastic

canvas piece **65** and insert inside handle (**D**). Pin around underside of handle so that interfacing and plastic canvas are contained within. Using a zipper foot, stitch around underside of handle (**E**). **NB: The handle 'filling' does not come to the bottom of the handle. This is so that you can stitch the handle to the bag with ease. Trim the seam allowance evenly.**

Step 3

Pin the handle to the bag front piece, centring over centre front, and machine-baste in place.

Step 4

Iron interfacing onto the back piece. Pin back piece to back lining piece, mark zipper placement onto interfacing side of back and set zipper in. Refer to **How to Set in a Back Zipper**, page 28. Remember to leave

zipper **open** after setting in, as you will turn the bag through this.

Step 5

Pin the interfaced front and back sections together, right sides of main fabric together. Stitch right around entire outside edge, through main bag pieces, including handle, leaving a ½in (13mm) seam allowance. **Leave lining piece free.** Clip into seam allowance around curved edges.

Step 6

Pin the remaining lining piece **63** to the back lining (which is now attached to the back via the zipper) and stitch pieces together at sides and lower edges, leaving an opening of around 5in (13cm) at centre of lower edge for turning. **NB: Gap must be large enough to get handle through.** Refer to **Lining a Bag with a Back Zipper**, page 29.

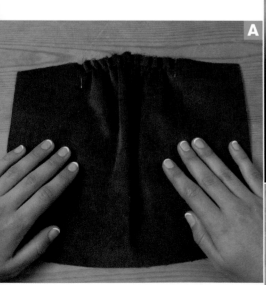

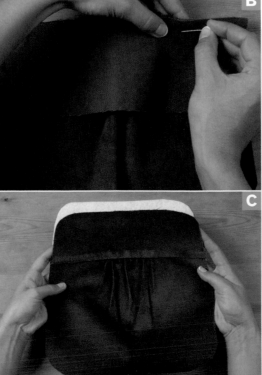

variations

If you are confident enough to stitch with leather, you could make the **handle** from **soft leather**. You could then also make the leaves of the **corsage** from toning leather, backed with felt. For tips on sewing leather see **veronica**, page 92.

To make the matching corsage

you will need

* 6 x 12in (15 x 31cm) of red or burgundy felt for roses
* 5 x 7in (13 x 18cm) of felt in two shades of grey for leaves
* three 6mm beads and three seed beads for flower centre
* one brooch backing bar with holes for sewing

cutting out

* Cut 1 x large petal **66** from red felt
* Cut 1 x small petal **67** from red felt
* Cut 1 x large leaf **68** from light grey felt
* Cut 1 x medium leaf **69** from each of light grey and dark grey felt
* Cut 1 x small leaf **70** from dark grey felt

Step 7

Turn the bag right side out through the opening in the bottom of the lining and the zipper. Push curved corners outwards. Slip-stitch the opening in the lining closed. Turn the lining into the bag and tuck well into the corners and curves. Do up the zipper, and press the bag using a cloth.

Step 1

Take each petal piece and gather up around inside curves (**F**). Curl into a flower shape and secure with a few stitches. Lay one piece on top of other and stitch together through the centre. Take a fine needle up through the centre of the flower, through a 6mm bead and a seed bead, then skip the seed bead and come back through the 6mm bead only and down through the flower (**G**). Repeat this for the other beads.

Step 2

Make leaves. Lay dark leaves on top of light and machine stitch together around edge of dark pieces, approximately ¼in (6mm) from the edge. Stitch the dart in the bottom of each finished leaf on the reverse side (**H**). Overlap finished leaves and stitch together. Stitch the rose to the leaves, covering gathers and raw edges. Finally, stitch the brooch bar onto the back of the corsage (**I**).

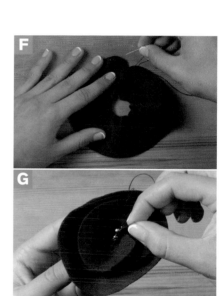

audrey

115

1950s

making **vintage** bags

vivien

1950s SMALL BOWBELLE BAG

Bows were a strong element in 1950s fashion and this little bag features an oversized bow that balances the shape of the bag whilst making a statement.

I like the idea of producing this bag from wool rather than sumptuous evening materials. A fabric with a harder edge counteracts the feminine aspect of the bow trim. This bag is large enough for use as a small but practical day bag. It would still translate well into an evening style and if you wanted to go all out for glamour, you could make this project entirely in silk brocade – think Ascot races or a grand spring wedding!

dimensions

Approximately 7in (18cm) deep by 10in (26cm) wide (excluding handle)

pattern pieces

71 72 73 74 75 76

pages 162–4

suggested fabrics

for main bag fabric:
wool flannel or tweed

for bag lining:
plain or patterned silk

you will need

* 22in (56cm) of tweed fabric, 36in (92cm) wide
* 9in (23cm) of lining fabric, 36in (92cm) wide
* 12in (31cm) of heavy weight sew-in interfacing, 36in (92cm) wide
* Fusible web 4 x 18in (10 x 46cm) for handle
* 18in (46cm) of velvet ribbon, 1½in (38mm) width for handle trim
* two pieces of craft interfacing (for snap stabilizers) 1½in (4cm) square
* one magnetic snap set
* one piece of plastic canvas to insert in base 1½ x 7¾in (4 x 20cm)
* 6 x 3in (15 x 8cm) of fusible web for bow centre

cutting out

* Cut 2 x piece **71** (front/back) from main fabric
* Cut 2 x piece **71** (front/back) from interfacing
* Cut 2 x piece **72** (facing) from main fabric
* Cut 2 x piece **73** (front/back lining) from lining fabric
* Cut 1 x piece **74** (handle) from main fabric on fold
* Cut 1 x piece **74** (handle) from fusible web on fold
* Cut 2 x piece **75** (main bow piece) from main fabric
* Cut 1 x piece **76** (bow centre) from main fabric and fusible web

making up instructions

Step 1
Pin front and back **71** sections to corresponding interfacing **71** pieces and baste-stitch together around outside edges. Refer to section on **Using Sew-in Interfacing**, page 17.

Step 2
Pin the two interfaced front/back sections right sides together. Stitch round sides and lower edges, leaving a ½in (13mm) seam allowance and leaving corners free. Trim the seam allowance back to around ⅜in (1cm) to cut down on bulk. Fold the lower corners of the bag matching seams, and stitch straight across to form gusset.

Step 3
Repeat this on the opposite corner. Turn bag right sides out and press.

Step 4
Make handle by ironing fusible web onto reverse side of handle piece and folding in long edges to centre. Fuse in place, then pin ribbon centrally onto handle, covering join. Machine stitch ribbon in place down both edges (**A**). Refer to **Self-fabric Handles**, page 20.

Step 5
On outside of bag, position handle at centre front and centre back, right sides of handle and bag together, having raw edges even. Pin and baste handle in place (**B**). **NB: You will have to take the handle under the bag and the bag will need to be folded up slightly whilst sewing.**

Step 6
Stitch lower edges of facing pieces **72** to upper edges of lining pieces **73** with right sides together. Press seam upwards. Refer to **How to Line a Top-opening Bag**, page 26.

Step 7
On facing pieces **72**, transfer snap marker positions and fix magnetic snaps using stabilizer interfacing squares. Refer to **Magnetic Snaps**, page 24. If using a fabric label, stitch this to one side of the assembled lining at this point (**C**).

Step 8
Stitch lining/facing pieces together at side and lower edges, leaving corners free and leaving a gap of around 5in (13cm) in the centre of the bottom for turning the bag through. Fold the lower corners of the lining matching seams, and stitch straight across to form gusset as you did for main bag.

Step 9
With right sides together, pin lining to bag with raw edges even, and baste together around upper edges. Pin and baste through all thicknesses, including handles. Stitch using a medium stitch length and leaving a ½ inch (13mm)

seam allowance. As this is a small bag with a narrow 'neck', this stage can be tricky, so stitch slowly and carefully, especially over the handle. Trim the seam back to around ³⁄₈in (1cm) to eliminate bulk and clip into the seam allowance near side seams.

Step 10

Turn the bag right side out through the opening in the lining. Insert plastic canvas into base, then slip-stitch the opening closed. Turn the lining into the bag.

Step 11

Roll the facing with your fingers so that it is not visible from the outside, then pin and hand-baste it in place around the upper edge of the bag. Top-stitch through all layers, about ¹⁄₂in (13mm) from the top of the bag, using a medium to long stitch length. Remember, the bag is small and quite tricky to access for top-stitching, so take extra care when sewing through

the bulkier areas. Close the bag and then give it a thorough press.

Step 12

Cut out bow pieces and assemble referring to section on **Making a Bow (Style 1: Angled Bow)**, page 35.

Step 13

Position bow at top edge of bag, centring on the handle. Hand-stitch in place with top edge of bow extending above upper edge of bag (**D**).

variations

If you have a pretty patterned **lining** that matches your main fabric well, you can omit the facing and line right to the **top** of the bag. For this, use pattern piece **71** front/back as your lining template, and cut two pieces. Trim about ½in (13mm) from top edge of both lining pieces and attach magnetic snaps to lining instead. Using facings makes a bag look very professional, but as the neck of this bag is quite small, if you are using thicker fabrics, lining to the top may be less bulky than using a facing.

vivien

119

1950s

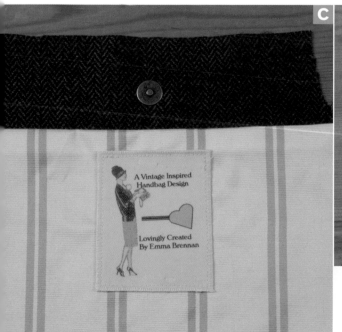

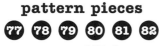

shirley

1950s TWO-TONE FLOWER TRIM SMALL BAG

Although this bag is small, it has found its way into the 1950s section because of its nice bucket shape and its flowery trims, which were very popular in this decade.

This bag features contrast side panels, a single wrist strap with contrasting underside and purchased ribbon blooms in a toning shade, backed with handmade leaves. It looks quite dressy, but the simple solid shape, especially when made up in functional tweed and fake suede, makes it a very serviceable day bag, just large enough to house the essentials.

dimensions

Approximately 7in (18cm) deep by 10in (26cm) wide (excluding handle)

pattern pieces

77 78 79 80 81 82

pages 165–6

suggested fabrics

for main bag fabric: patterned wool tweed

for contrast panels: fake suede

for bag lining: plain or patterned silk

you will need

* 18in (46cm) of tweed fabric, 36in (92cm) wide
* 18in (46cm) of contrast fabric, 18in (46cm) wide for side panels/handle
* 9in (23cm) of lining fabric, 36in (92cm) wide
* 12in (31cm) of heavy weight sew-in interfacing, 36in (92cm) wide
* fusible web 7 x 18in (18 x 46cm) for handle
* two 1½in (4cm) square pieces of craft interfacing (for snap stabilizers)
* one magnetic snap set
* piece of plastic canvas to insert in base 1½ x 7¾in (4 x 20cm)
* three purchased ribbon flowers for trim
* approximately 36in (92cm) of narrow ribbon (¼in (6mm) wide) for the leaves

cutting out

* Cut 1 x piece **77** (front centre panel) from main fabric
* Cut 2 x piece **78** (front side panel) from contrast fabric
* Cut 1 x piece **79** (back) from main fabric
* Cut 2 x piece **79** (back) from interfacing
* Cut 2 x piece **80** (facing) from main fabric
* Cut 2 x piece **81** (front/back lining) from lining fabric
* Cut 1 x piece **82** (handle) from main fabric on fold
* Cut 1 x piece **82** (handle) from contrast fabric on fold
* Cut 2 x piece **82** (handle) from fusible web on fold

making up instructions

Step 1

Pin front centre panel piece **77** and front side panel pieces **78** together along edges marked with dotted line on pattern templates (**A**). Baste and machine stitch together, leaving a ½in (13mm) seam allowance. Press seams toward outer edges.

Step 2

Pin assembled front piece to one interfacing piece **79** and baste together around outside edges. Refer to **Using Sew-in Interfacing**, page 17. Machine stitch (using a long stitch length) along the seams of the front panels (**B**).

Step 3

Cut the narrow ribbon into six equal lengths of around 6in (15cm). Make leaves by twisting and folding as in pictures (**C**) and (**D**). You will need two leaves for each flower. Secure folds with a few stitches, then stitch leaves to bag centre front at positions marked with an X on the pattern template. Layer one leaf on top of the other in a cross shape (**E**).

Step 4

Hand-stitch the three ribbon roses down the centre front panel positioned over the leaves (**F**).

Step 5

Pin the back section to the corresponding back interfacing piece and baste-stitch together around outside edges.

Step 6

Pin the two interfaced front/back sections right sides together. Stitch around sides and lower edges, leaving a ½in (13mm) seam allowance, and leaving the corners free. Trim the seams back to ⅜in (1cm) to cut down on bulk. Fold the lower corners of the bag matching seams, and stitch straight across to form gusset.

Step 7

Repeat this on the opposite corner. Turn bag right sides out and press.

Step 8

Make handle by ironing fusible web onto reverse side of both handle pieces. Fold in long edges to centre and fuse in place. Pin handle sections wrong sides together, with folded edges even. Stitch together down both long edges approximately ¼in (6mm) from the edge. Refer to **Self-fabric Handles**, page 20.

Step 9

On outside of bag, position handle at centre front and centre back. With raw edges even, pin handle to bag and baste in place. Note that you will have to take the handle under the bag and the bag will need to be folded up slightly whilst sewing.

A

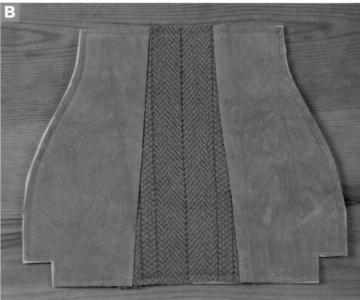

B

making **vintage** bags

Step 10

Stitch lower edges of facing pieces **80** to upper edges of lining pieces **81** with right sides together. Refer to **How to Line a Top-opening Bag**, page 26.

Step 11

On facing pieces **80**, transfer snap marker positions and fix magnetic snaps using stabilizer interfacing squares. Refer to **Magnetic Snaps**, page 24.

Step 12

Stitch lining/facing pieces together at side and lower edges, leaving corners free and leaving a gap of around 5in (13cm) in the centre of the bottom for turning the bag through. Fold the lower corners of the lining matching seams, and stitch straight across to form gusset as you did for main bag.

Step 13

With right sides together, pin lining to bag with raw edges even, and baste together around upper edges. Pin and baste through all thicknesses, including handle. Stitch using a medium stitch length and leaving a 1/2in (13mm) seam allowance. As this is a small bag with a narrow 'neck', this stage can be tricky, so stitch slowly and carefully, especially over the handle. Trim the seam back to around 3/8in (1cm) to eliminate bulk and clip into the seam allowance near side seams.

Step 14

Turn the bag right side out through the opening in the lining. Insert plastic canvas into base, then slip-stitch the opening closed. Turn the lining into the bag.

Step 15

Roll the facing with your fingers so that it is not visible from the outside pin and hand-baste it in place round upper edge of bag. Top-stitch through all layers, about 1/2in (13mm) from the top of the bag, using a medium to long stitch length. The bag is small and quite tricky to access for top-stitching, so take extra care when sewing through the bulkier areas. Close the bag and then give it a press.

shirley

123

1950s

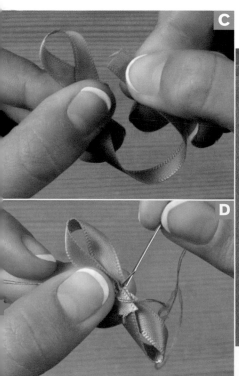

making **vintage** bags

peggy

1950s STRIPED BOW BAG WITH STRAIGHT HANDLE

This bag reminds me of sunny holidays by the sea, the deckchair stripes evoking just a touch of retro Riviera glamour. The nice roomy shape is evocative of 1950s silhouettes and offers a very practical-sized bag for modern use. The bow trim is also very 1950s.

The subtle hues of the stripes used in this project add to the faded vintage feel and the added bonus of choosing a canvas weight fabric means that it is not necessary to interface or stiffen it. To keep the look of the bag simple, I've chosen to use natural wooden buttons as a trim to tie in with the handle – I've also used an unfussy quilted calico lining.

you will need

* 20in (51cm) of main fabric, 54in (138cm) wide
* 18in (46cm) of quilted lining fabric, 48in (122cm) wide
* 9in (23cm) zipper
* one piece of plastic canvas 11½ x 3½in (29 x 9cm) for base
* one long pole-shaped wooden handle with end knobs, minimum length 12in (31cm) including knobs
* two wooden buttons for tab trims
* one piece of fusible web for bow centre, exactly 2 x 4in (5 x 10cm)

cutting out

* Cut 2 x piece **83** (front/back) from main fabric on fold
* Cut 2 x piece **84** (front/back lining) from quilted lining fabric on fold
* Cut 4 x piece **85** (handle carrier tabs) from main fabric
* Cut 1 x piece **86** (bow) from main fabric
* Cut 1 x piece **87** (bow centre) from main fabric and fusible web

dimensions

Approximately 14in (36cm) deep by 15½in (39cm) wide (excluding handle)

pattern pieces

83 **84** **85** **86** **87**

pages 167–9

suggested fabrics

for main bag fabric:
canvas weight striped fabric in faded tones

for bag lining:
quilted cotton lining fabric

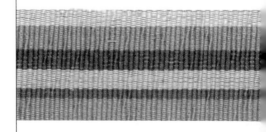

making up instructions

Step 1

Make handle carrier tabs. Place two tab **85** pieces right sides together and stitch round side and bottom edges, leaving top edge open for turning. Clip corners (**A**) and turn right side out. Top-stitch about ½in (13mm) from the edge. Repeat for other tab.

Step 2

Place tabs on front as shown in picture (**B**), pin and stitch in place along top edge.

Step 3

Pin back piece **83** to back lining piece **84**, right sides together, mark zip placement onto reverse side of back and set zip in. Refer to **How to Set in a Back Zipper**, page 28. Remember to **leave zipper open** after setting in, as you will turn the bag through this.

Step 4

Pin the front and back **83** sections right sides together. Stitch right around the top and side edges, and along the bottom edge, leaving the corners free. Stitch through main bag pieces, including handle carrier tabs, pivoting at corners and leaving a ½in (13mm) seam allowance. **Leave lining piece free.** Refer to **Lining a Bag with a Back Zipper**, page 29.

Step 5

Clip curve and corners at upper edge. Fold the lower corners of the bag matching seams, and stitch straight across to form gusset. You will have to access the corners through the zipper opening.

Step 6

Pin the remaining front lining **84** piece to the back lining (which is now attached to the back of the bag via the zip) and stitch right around the top and side edges,

and along the bottom edge, leaving the corners free and leaving an opening of around 6in (15cm) at the centre of the lower edge for turning. Fold lower corners of bag lining, matching the seams, and stitch straight across to form gusset.

Step 7

Turn the bag right side out, first through the opening in the bottom of the lining and then through the zipper. Push corners outwards, pull tabs upwards, shape curved edges and press top of bag thoroughly. Insert plastic canvas in to base of bag and slip-stitch the opening in lining closed. Turn the lining into the bag; do up zipper and press bag again.

Step 8

Attach the handle. Fold handle carrier tabs over handle and pin in place. The tabs must sit tightly around the handle and the knobs on the end need to be sufficiently

A B

making **vintage** bags

large enough to stop the handle from slipping off. Secure the handle in place by hand stitching both sides of each tab, close up against the underneath of the handle (**C**).

Step 9

Make bow. If you are using a canvas weight material the bow will only need to be single thickness. Cut out one bow shape using the template. Neaten the outside edge of the bow by stitching around it with a satin stitch or close zigzag stitch. Make bow centre and complete the rest of the bow by referring back to the detailed instructions in section on **Making a Bow (Style 2: Rounded Bow)**, page 36 (**D**).

Step 10

Hand-stitch the bow in a central position, close to the curved top edge of the bag front.

Step 11

Stitch a button each side on the flap part of the handle carriers (**E**).

variations

This bag uses a straight **wooden handle**. For the bag in the main photograph (page 124), I have used a handle that was specially made for me by a wood-turner friend. You can however, buy straight handles which have **rounded knobs** at

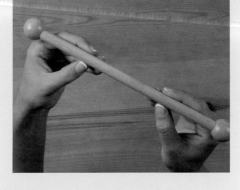

each end, one of which comes off so that you can slip the handle though the tabs after you've stitched them. This makes it a little less awkward to sew and if your fabric is not too thick, you can even machine stitch the tabs as I have for **gloria** (page 130). Once the tabs are stitched into loops, the handle can be slipped through and the end knob secured in place with glue.

peggy

127

1950s

C

D

E

making **vintage** bags

making up instructions

To make the matching purse

Use the standard purse template **91** and for the bow, use pieces **86** and **87** from the Peggy pattern templates.

you will need

* 8in (21cm) of main fabric, 20in (51cm) wide

* 8in (21cm) of quilted lining fabric, 16in (41cm) wide

* one 6in (15cm) zipper

* one piece of fusible web exactly 2 x 4in (5 x10cm) for bow centre

cutting out

* Cut 2 x piece purse template **91** (front/back) from main fabric

* Cut 2 x piece purse template **91** (front/back) from quilted lining fabric

* Cut 1 x piece **86** (bow) from main fabric

* Cut 1 x piece **87** (bow centre) from main fabric and fusible web

If you are using finer thinner material for both the bag and purse, you may need to make a 'double thickness' bow. If this is the case, add a ½in (13mm) seam allowance to piece **86** (bow) when cutting out. Make up following the rounded bow instructions, page 36.

Step 1
Assemble purse referring to **Making Matching Purses**, page 31.

Step 2
Make bow following instructions for bow in main bag.

Step 3
Hand-stitch bow in central position near top edge of purse. Place so that the rounded top of the bow sits slightly above the top edge of the purse.

peggy

129

1950s

gloria

1950s PICTURE BAG WITH ROPE HANDLE

This bag is an amalgamation of styles. Using the same pattern pieces as the previous project (Peggy, page 124), it combines the vintage-look ticking striped cotton, the old-fashioned braid buttons and tassel cord handle, and a 1950s feel photo appliqué.

I've chosen an image of a Victorian boot to adorn my bag, but more modern images or vintage photographs would work equally well. The black braid trim around the picture gives the impression of a frame and the tiny roses at each corner lend a feminine finishing touch. The choice of almost monochromatic shades also adds to the vintage feel while leaving it practical enough for modern use. Photo image bags have become extremely popular in recent years and offer a great way to personalize your accessories even further.

dimensions

Approximately 14in (36cm) deep by 15½in (39cm) wide (excluding handle)

pattern pieces

88 **89** **90** pages 167–9

suggested fabrics

for main bag fabric:
medium weight ticking striped fabric

for bag lining:
quilted cotton lining fabric

you will need

✻ 20in (51cm) of main fabric, 54in (140cm) wide

✻ 20in (51cm) of firm weight sew-in interfacing, 48in (122cm) wide

✻ 18in (46cm) of quilted lining fabric, 48in (122cm) wide

✻ 9in (23cm) zipper

✻ Piece of plastic canvas 11½ x 3½in (29 x 9cm) for base

✻ 7 x 20in (18 x 51cm) of iron-on interfacing for handle carrier tabs

✻ 60in (154cm) of twisted rope cording for handle

✻ a cut-out or transfer image in size of your choice printed onto plain cotton fabric

✻ approximately 36in (92cm) of gimp braid or ribbon (enough to frame your chosen image)

✻ two braid-covered buttons

✻ four small ribbon roses

cutting out

✻ Cut 2 x piece **88** (front/back) from main fabric on fold

✻ Cut 2 x piece **88** (front/back) from sew-in interfacing on fold

✻ Cut 2 x piece **89** (front/back lining) from quilted lining fabric on fold

✻ Cut 4 x piece **90** (handle carrier tabs) from main fabric

✻ Cut 4 x piece **90** (handle carrier tabs) from iron-on interfacing

making up instructions

Step 1
Pin front and back 88 sections to corresponding front and back 88 interfacing sections and baste-stitch together. Refer to **Sew-in Interfacing**, page 17.

Step 2
Take your image (now printed onto fabric) and position in a central place on the bag front piece. Pin and baste in place, then machine stitch around outside of image about ¼in (6mm) from the edge.

Step 3
Pin braid around image, ensuring that all raw edges are covered (**A**). Starting at the centre bottom of the image, curve braid around the corners and pin diagonally into corners to secure. When you have reached the point where you started, tuck end of braid under to neaten. Baste then stitch both edges of the braid to secure. Hand-stitch a ribbon rose at each corner. **NB: If you are using a**

'transfer' image, do not iron the image directly at any stage.

Step 4
Make handle tabs. Iron interfacing onto reverse side of each tab piece. Place two tab 90 pieces right sides together and stitch round side and bottom edges, leaving top edge open for turning. Clip corners and turn right side out. Top-stitch about ½in (13mm) from the edge. Repeat for other tab.

Step 5
Place tabs on front and stitch in place along top edge.

Step 6
Pin back piece 88 to back lining piece 89, right sides together, mark zip placement onto reverse interfaced side of back and set zip in. Refer to **How to Set in a Back Zipper,** page 28. Remember to leave the zipper **open** after setting in, as you will turn the bag through this later.

Step 7
Pin front and back sections right sides together. Stitch right around top and side edges, and along the bottom edge, leaving corners free. Stitch through main bag pieces, including handle carrier tabs, pivoting at corners and leaving a ½in (13mm) seam allowance. Ensure that you leave the lining piece free. Refer to **Lining a Bag with a Back Zipper**, page 29.

Step 8
Clip curve at top and clip corners. Fold the lower corners of the bag matching seams, and stitch straight across to form gusset. You will have to access the corners through the zipper opening.

Step 9
Pin the remaining front lining piece to the back lining (which is now attached to the back of the bag via the zip) and stitch right around the top and side edges, and along the bottom edge, leaving the corners

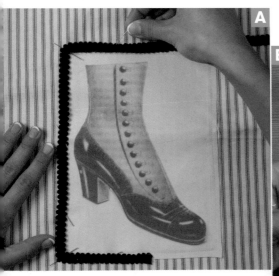

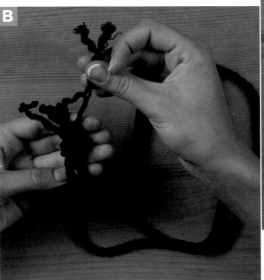

free and leaving an opening of around 6in (15cm) at centre of lower edge for turning. Fold the lower corners of the bag lining matching seams, and stitch straight across to form gusset.

Step 10

Turn bag right side out, first through the opening in the bottom of the lining and then through the zipper. Push corners outwards, pull tabs upwards, shape curved edges and press top of bag thoroughly. Insert plastic canvas in to base of bag and slip-stitch the opening in lining closed. Turn the lining into the bag; do up zipper and press bag again, avoiding the transfer image.

Step 11

Make the handle. Fold the twisted cord rope in half and tie the cut ends together in a tight overhand knot, approximately 3½in (9cm) from the ends. Untwist and unravel the ends of the rope to form a tassel (**B**).

Step 12

Fold handle carrier tabs over the double thickness of cord rope, gauge the depth of the loops and pin in place either side. The tabs should sit tightly against the rope and the knots need to be big enough so that the handle cannot slip off. Pull the knot up against the left-hand side tab. The folded end of the rope should be hanging from the other side of the right tab. Stitch the tabs in place using a zipper foot (**C**). You should stitch in the seam line from the reverse side of the bag. Tie a knot approximately 3½in (9cm) from the folded end of rope, cut the loop and form a tassel as you did with the other end (**D**, **E**). Pull the second knot close up against the right tab.

Step 13

Stitch a braid-covered button each side of the top of the bag, on the flap part of the handle carriers.

For this particular bag I have used a transfer image produced on a home computer. For information on other options, refer to **Photo Print Bags**, page 37.

This particular image of a boot was taken from a book of copyright-free illustrations dating from the early 1900s. There are several books of this type on the market, providing a rich source of vintage images for small scale reproduction. I scanned this image into a PC, enlarged it and printed it onto transfer paper. I then ironed it onto plain cream cotton drill fabric.

For this project, remember to vary the quantity of braid needed to edge the image according to the size of image you choose.

gloria

1950s

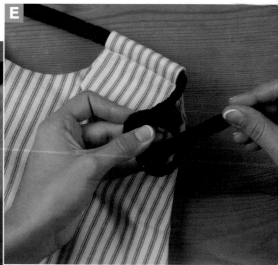

making **vintage** bags

① ② ③ **clara**

② **clara** appliqué strip

③ join edges at dotted lines

clara handle carrier

join edges at dotted lines

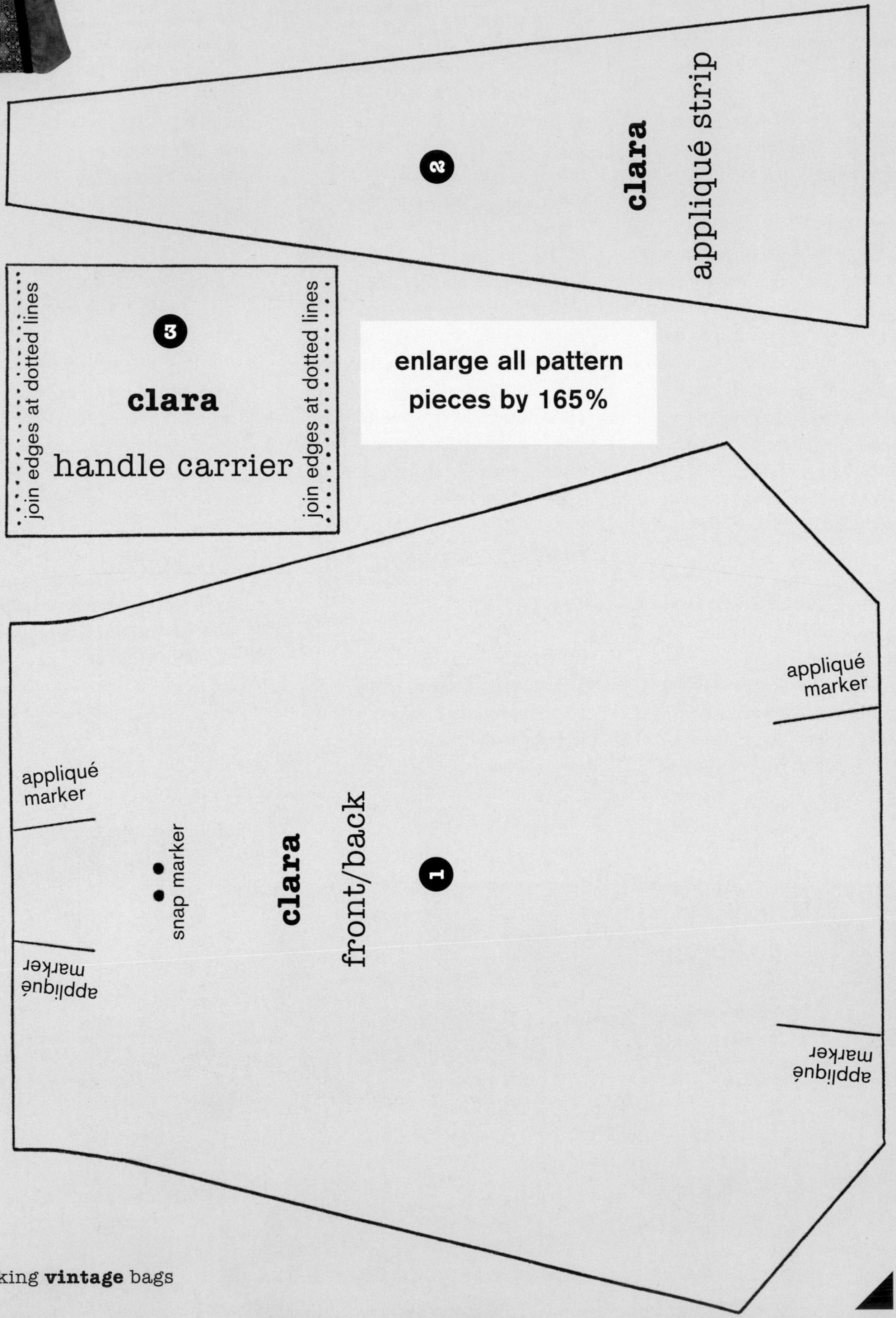

enlarge all pattern pieces by 165%

appliqué marker

appliqué marker

snap marker

appliqué marker

clara front/back

①

appliqué marker

when photocopying, align dotted rule with top edge of glass

making **vintage** bags

lucille ❹ ❺

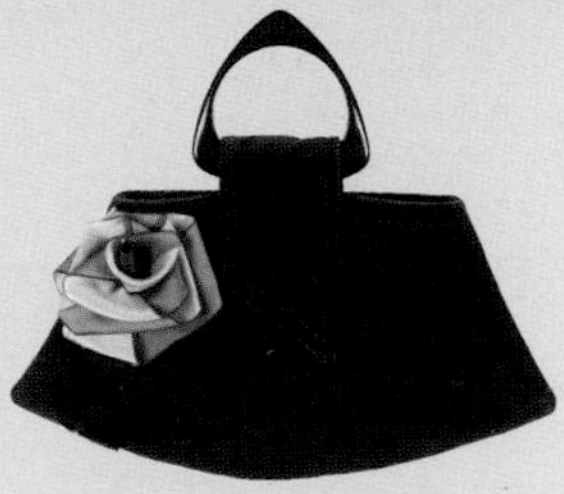

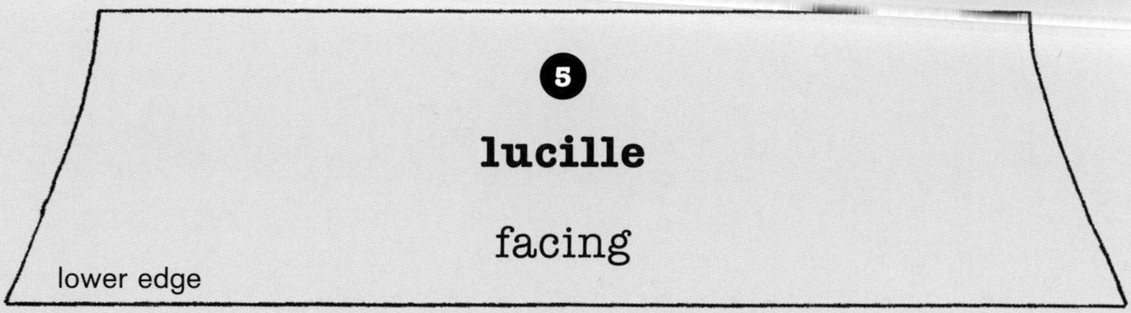
5
lucille
facing
lower edge

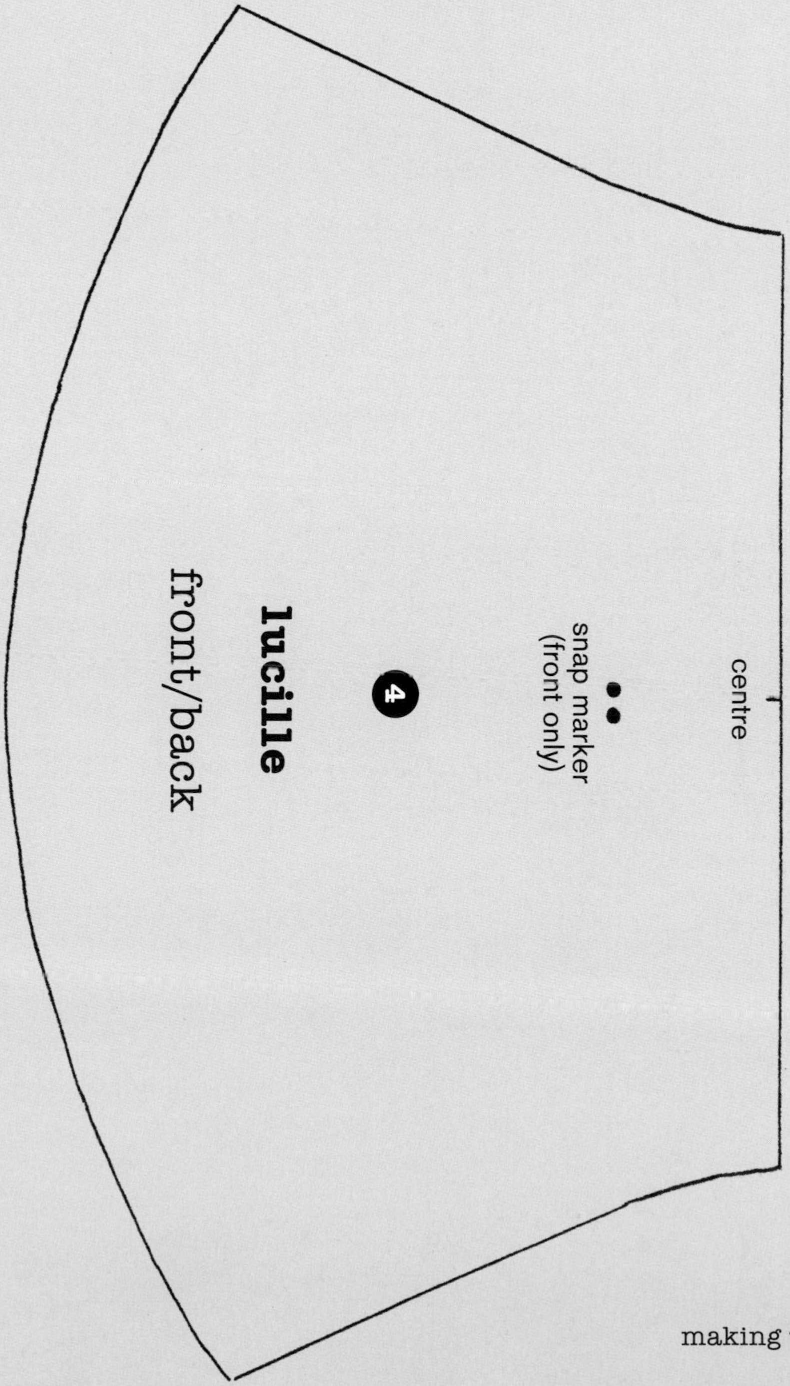
4
lucille
front/back
snap marker
(front only)
centre

enlarge all pattern pieces by 165%

6 7 8 lucille

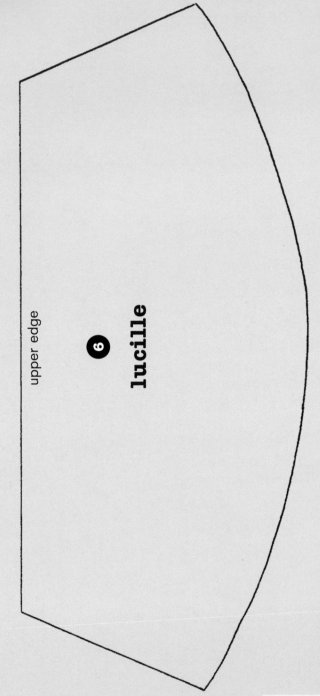

upper edge

6 lucille

7

lucille

snap marker
(underside only)

• •

8

lucille

handle
carrier

join edges at dotted lines

join edges at dotted lines

enlarge all pattern
pieces by 165%

when photocopying, align dotted rule with top edge of glass

virginia ⑨ ⑩

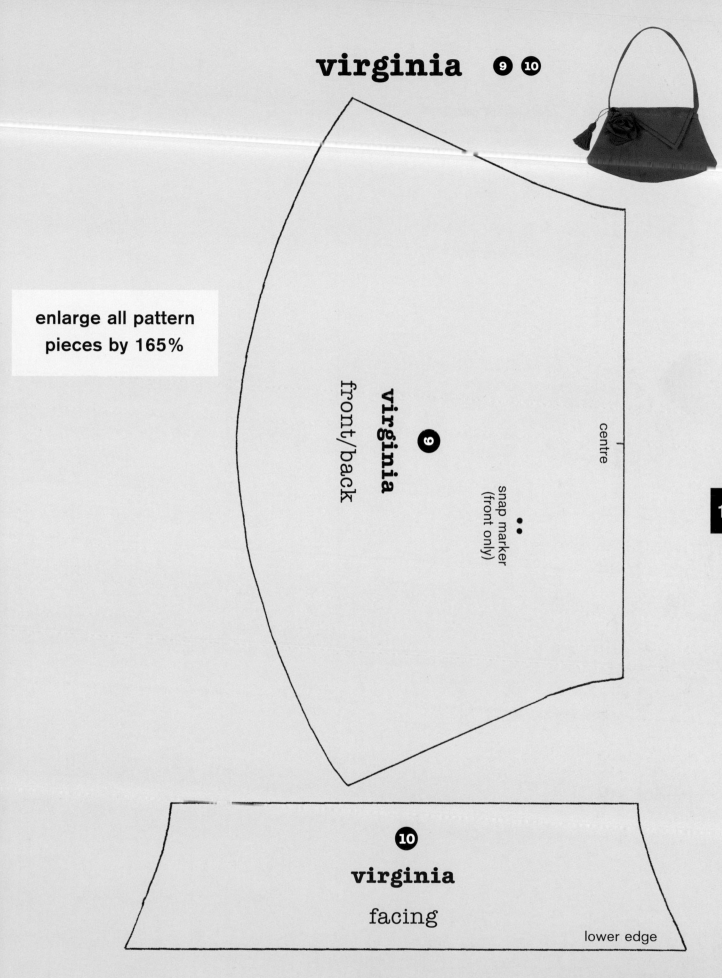

enlarge all pattern
pieces by 165%

virginia
front/back

⑨

centre

snap marker
(front only)

⑩

virginia

facing

lower edge

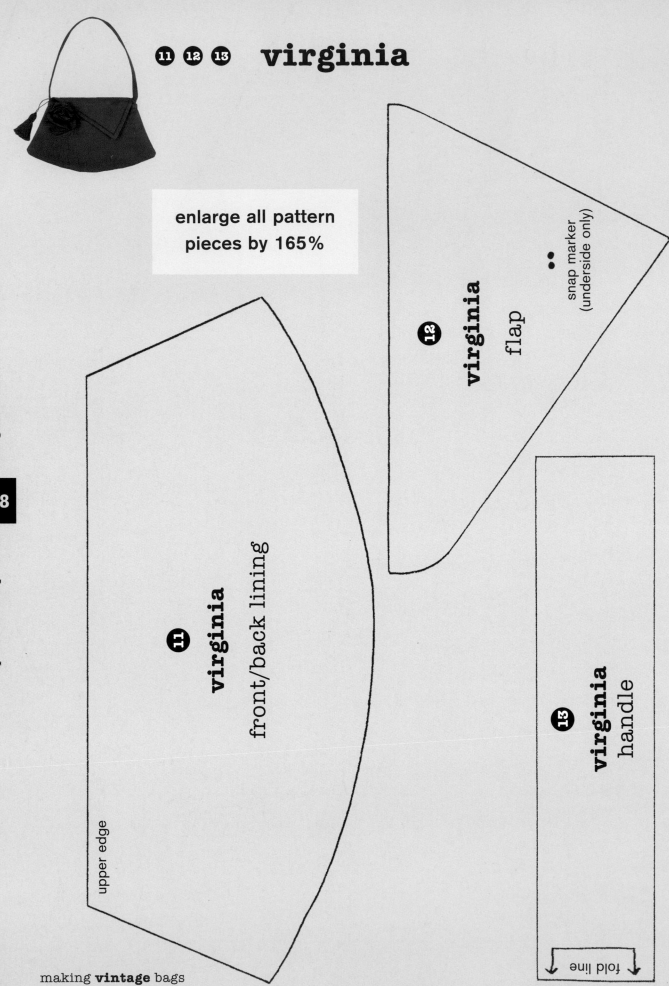

11 12 13 **virginia**

enlarge all pattern pieces by 165%

virginia
flap

12

snap marker
(underside only)

virginia
front/back lining

11

upper edge

virginia
handle

13

fold line

when photocopying, align dotted rule with top edge of glass

dorothy / evelyn ⑭ ⑱

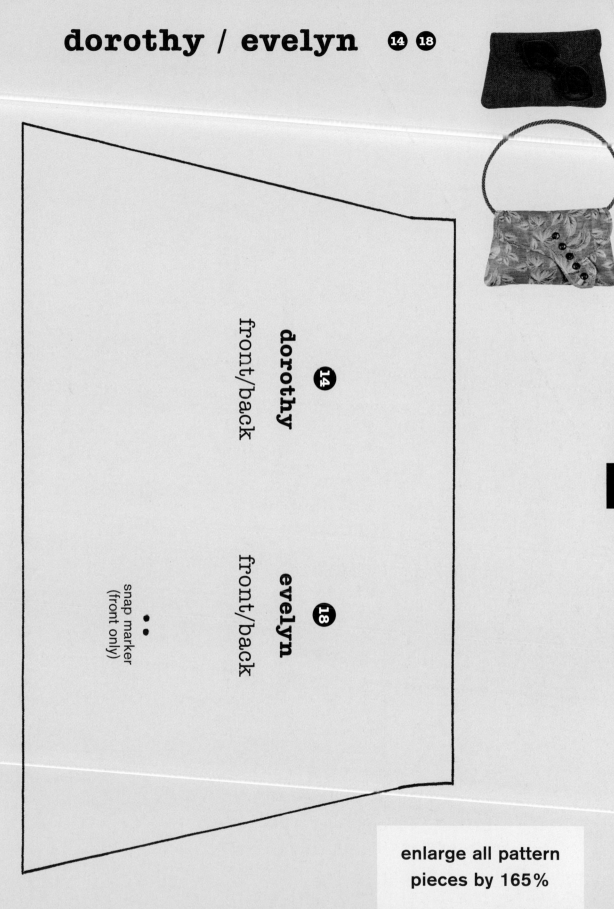

dorothy
front/back

⑭

evelyn
front/back

⑱

snap marker
(front only)

enlarge all pattern
pieces by 165%

⑮ ⑯ ⑰ ⑲ dorothy / evelyn

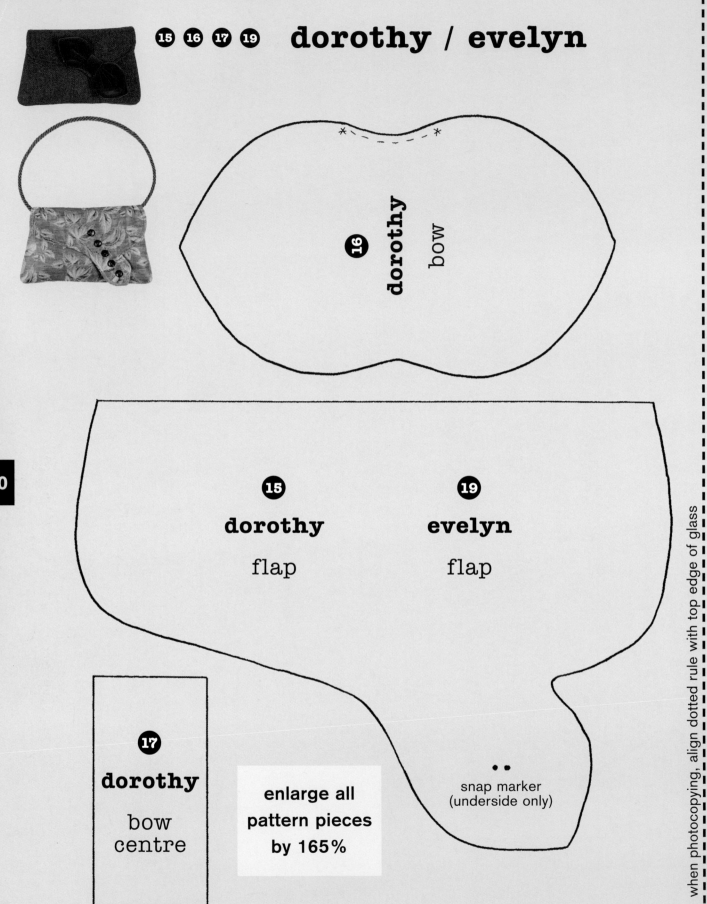

⑯ **dorothy** bow

⑮ **dorothy** flap

⑲ **evelyn** flap

⑰ **dorothy** bow centre

enlarge all pattern pieces by 165%

snap marker (underside only)

when photocopying, align dotted rule with top edge of glass

doris ② ②

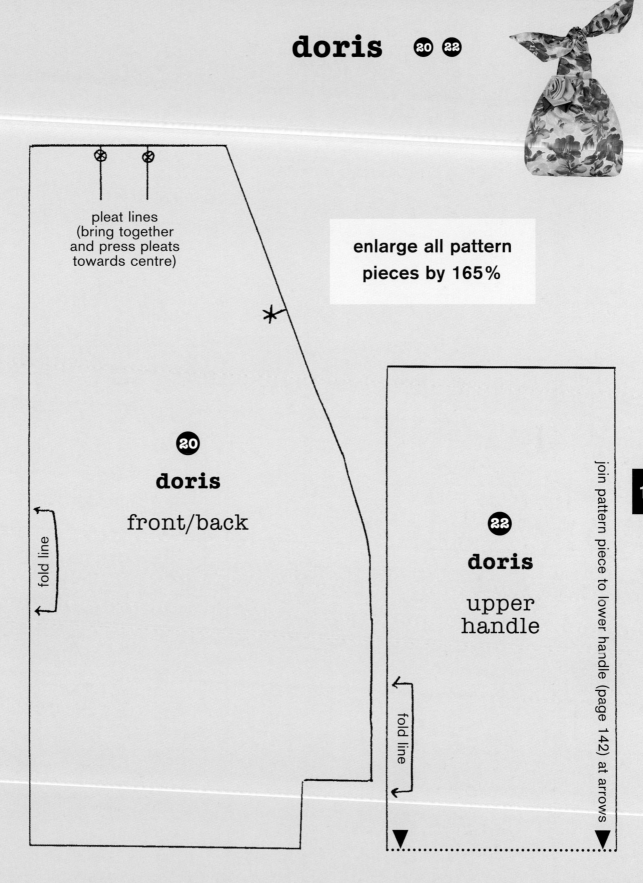

pleat lines
(bring together
and press pleats
towards centre)

**enlarge all pattern
pieces by 165%**

②

doris

front/back

fold line

②

doris

upper
handle

fold line

join pattern piece to lower handle (page 142) at arrows

pattern templates

making **vintage** *bags*

21 22 doris

enlarge all pattern
pieces by 165%

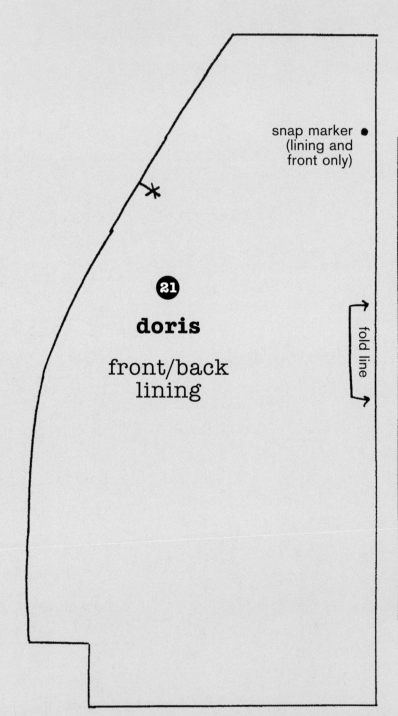

pattern templates

snap marker ●
(lining and
front only)

21

doris

front/back
lining

fold line

22

doris

lower
handle

join pattern piece to upper handle (page 141) at arrows

when photocopying, align dotted rule with top edge of glass

making **vintage** bags

nancy ㉓ ㉕ ㉖

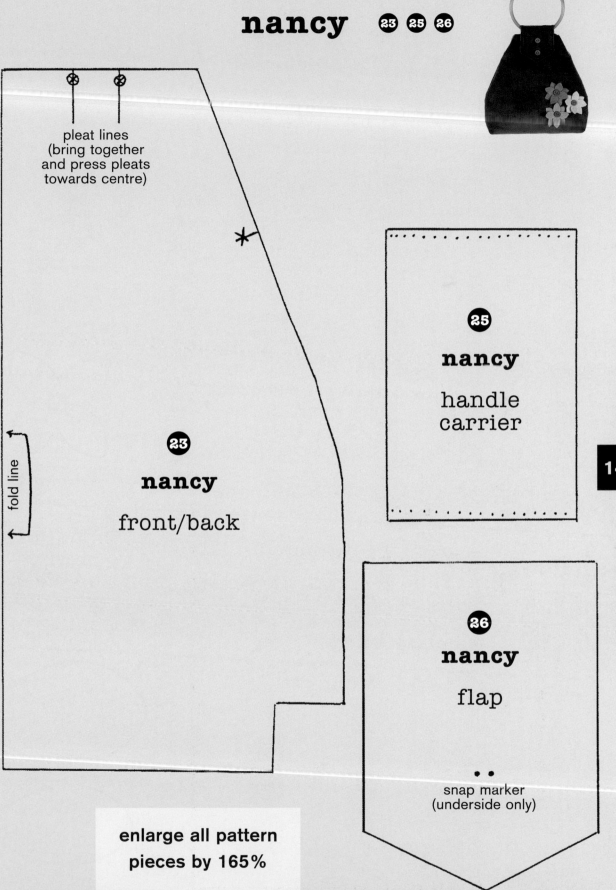

pleat lines
(bring together
and press pleats
towards centre)

fold line

㉓

nancy

front/back

㉕

nancy

handle
carrier

㉖

nancy

flap

• •

snap marker
(underside only)

enlarge all pattern
pieces by 165%

143

24 27 **nancy**

enlarge all pattern
pieces by 165%

144

snap marker ●
(lining and
front only)

fold line

24

nancy

front/back
lining

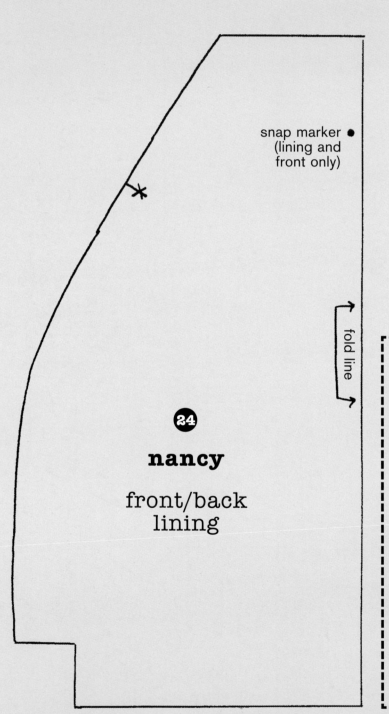

nancy

flower
appliqué

27

nancy

leaf appliqués for
matching purse

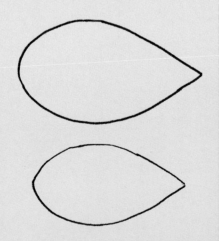

when photocopying, align dotted rule with top edge of glass

lois ㉘

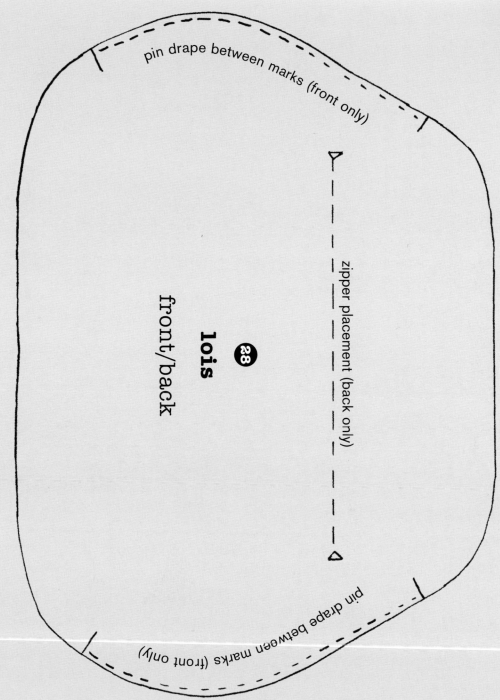

pin drape between marks (front only)

zipper placement (back only)

lois ㉘
front/back

pin drape between marks (front only)

㉙ ㉚ ㉝ **lois / rita**

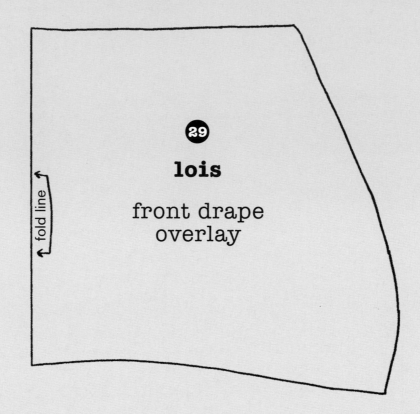

㉙

lois

front drape
overlay

← fold line →

enlarge all pattern
pieces by 165%

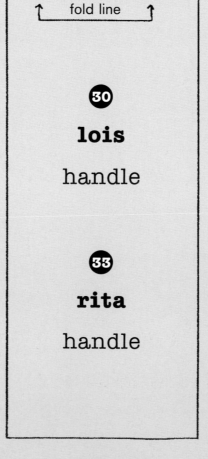

← fold line →

㉚

lois

handle

㉝

rita

handle

making **vintage** bags

when photocopying, align dotted rule with top edge of glass

rita ③① ③⑤

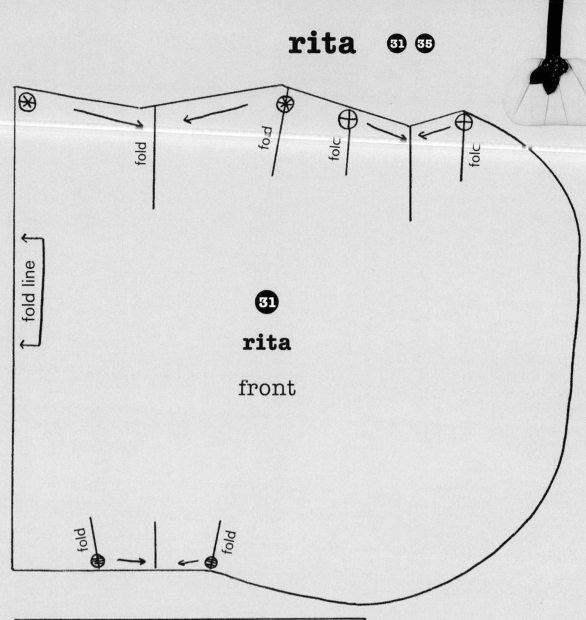

fold

fold

fold

fold

fold

fold line

③①

rita

front

fold

fold

③⑤

enlarge all pattern pieces by 165%

rita

fabric leaf

pattern templates

32 34 **rita**

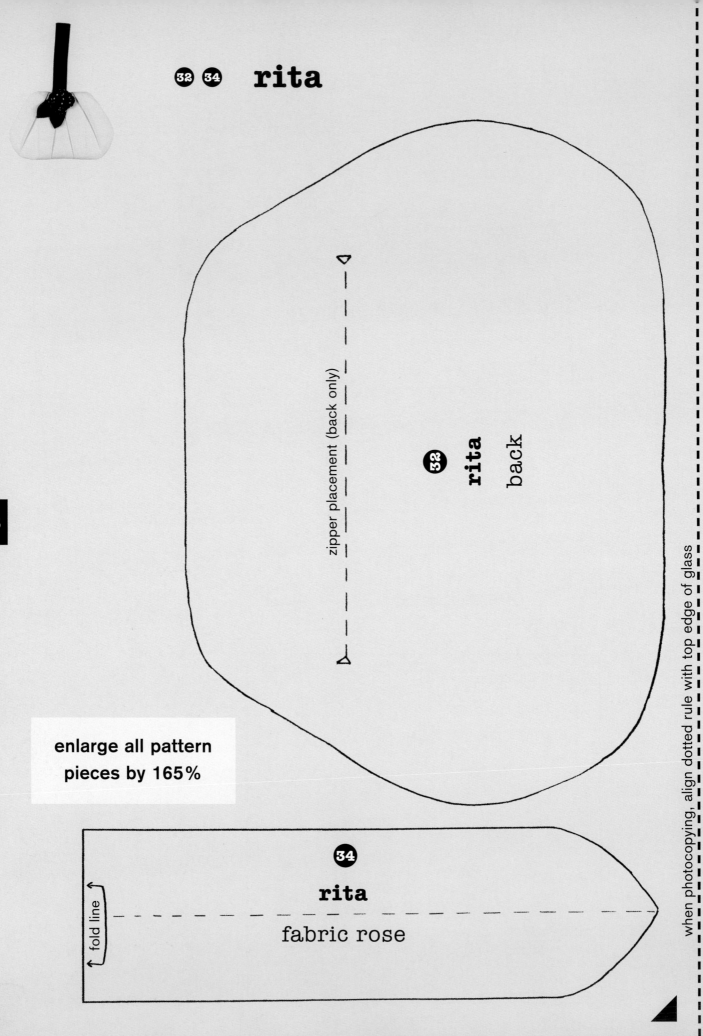

zipper placement (back only)

32

rita

back

enlarge all pattern
pieces by 165%

34

rita

fabric rose

fold line

when photocopying, align dotted rule with top edge of glass

marion ㊱ ㊲

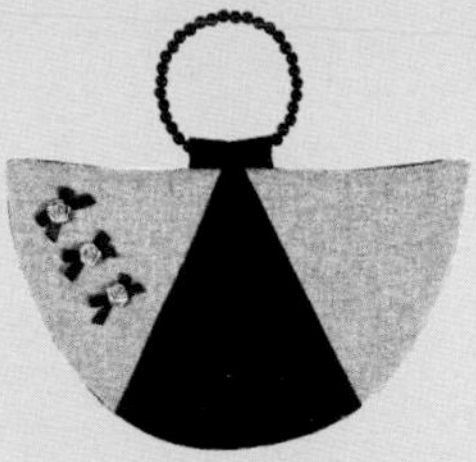

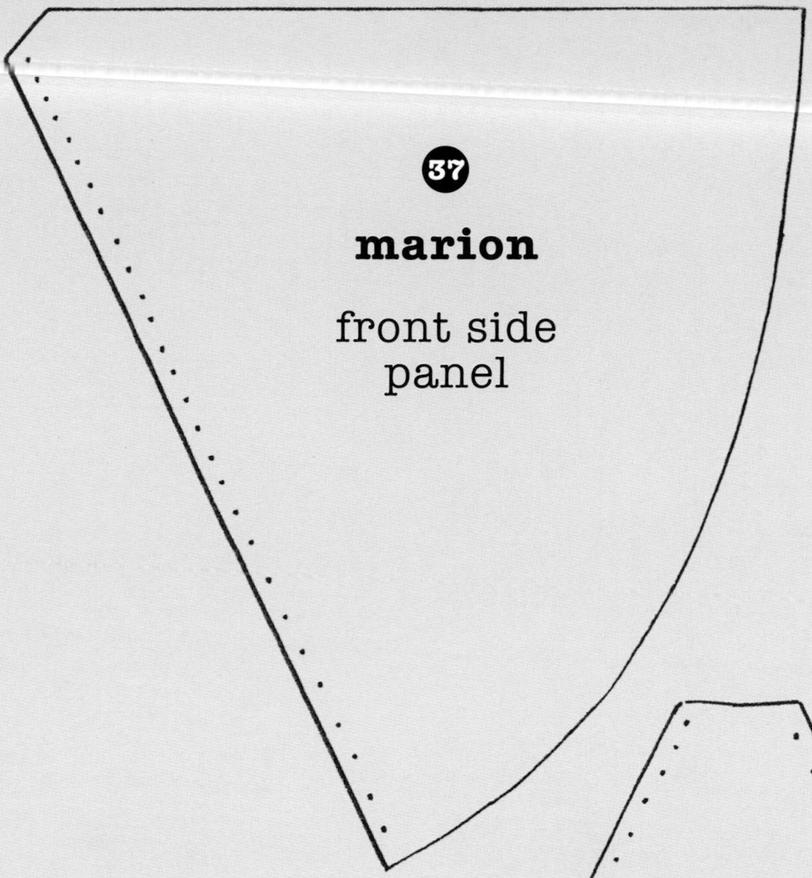
㊲
marion
front side panel

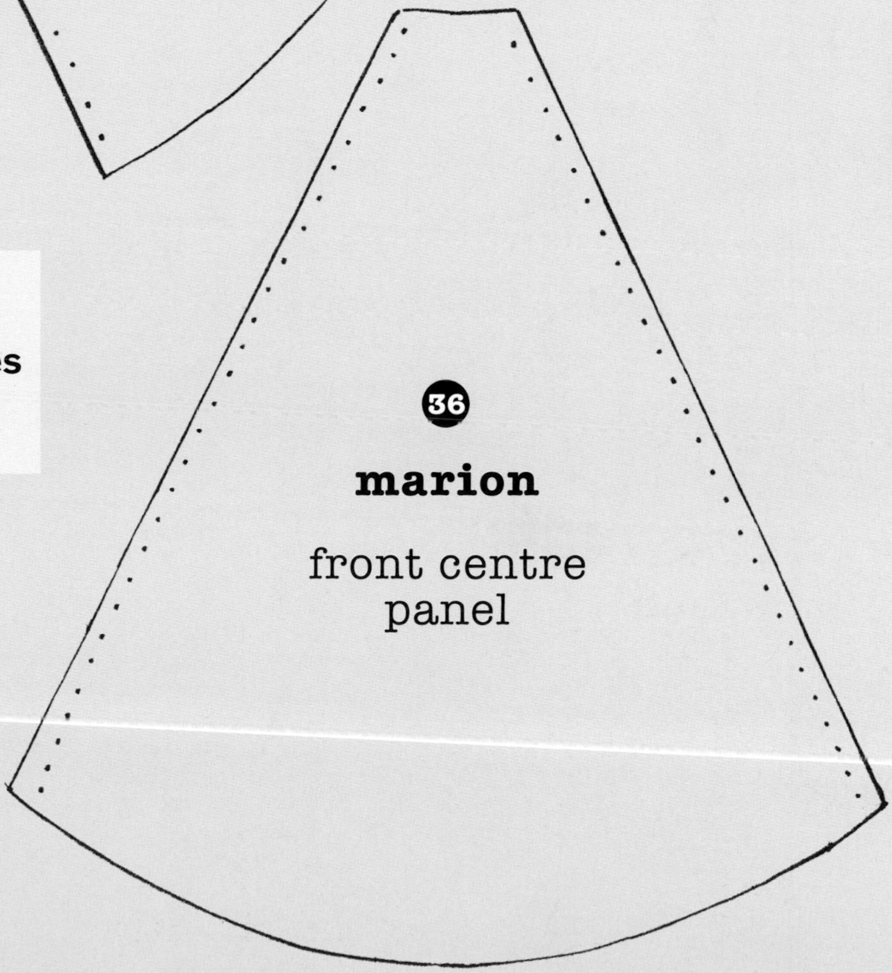
㊱
marion
front centre panel

enlarge all pattern pieces by 165%

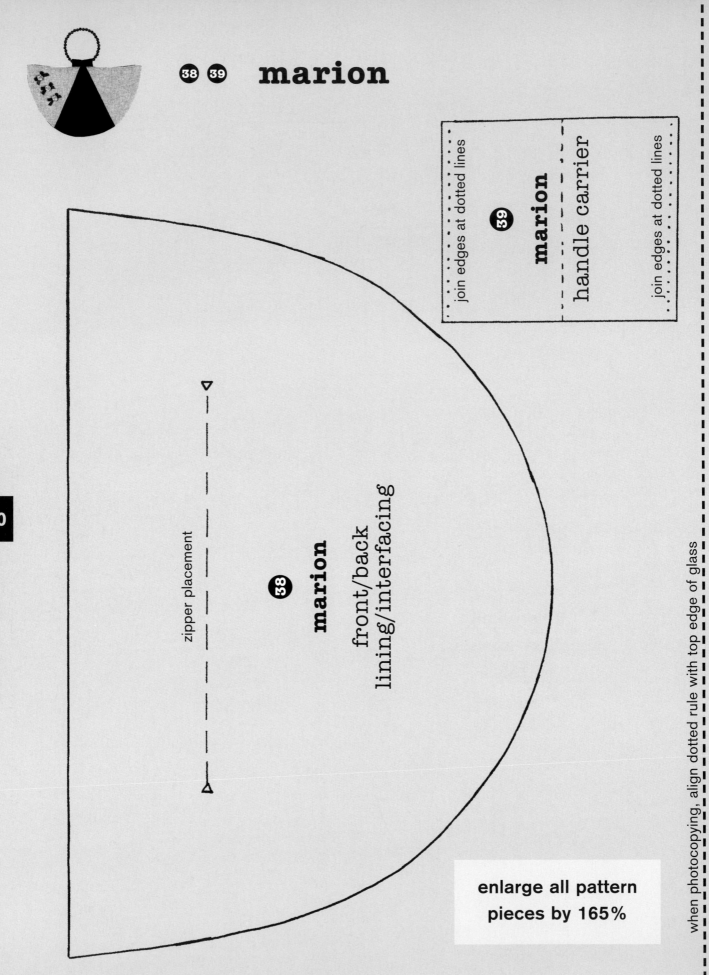

38 39 **marion**

join edges at dotted lines

39

marion

handle carrier

join edges at dotted lines

zipper placement

38

marion

front/back
lining/interfacing

**enlarge all pattern
pieces by 165%**

when photocopying, align dotted rule with top edge of glass

martha ④⓪

enlarge all pattern
pieces by 165%

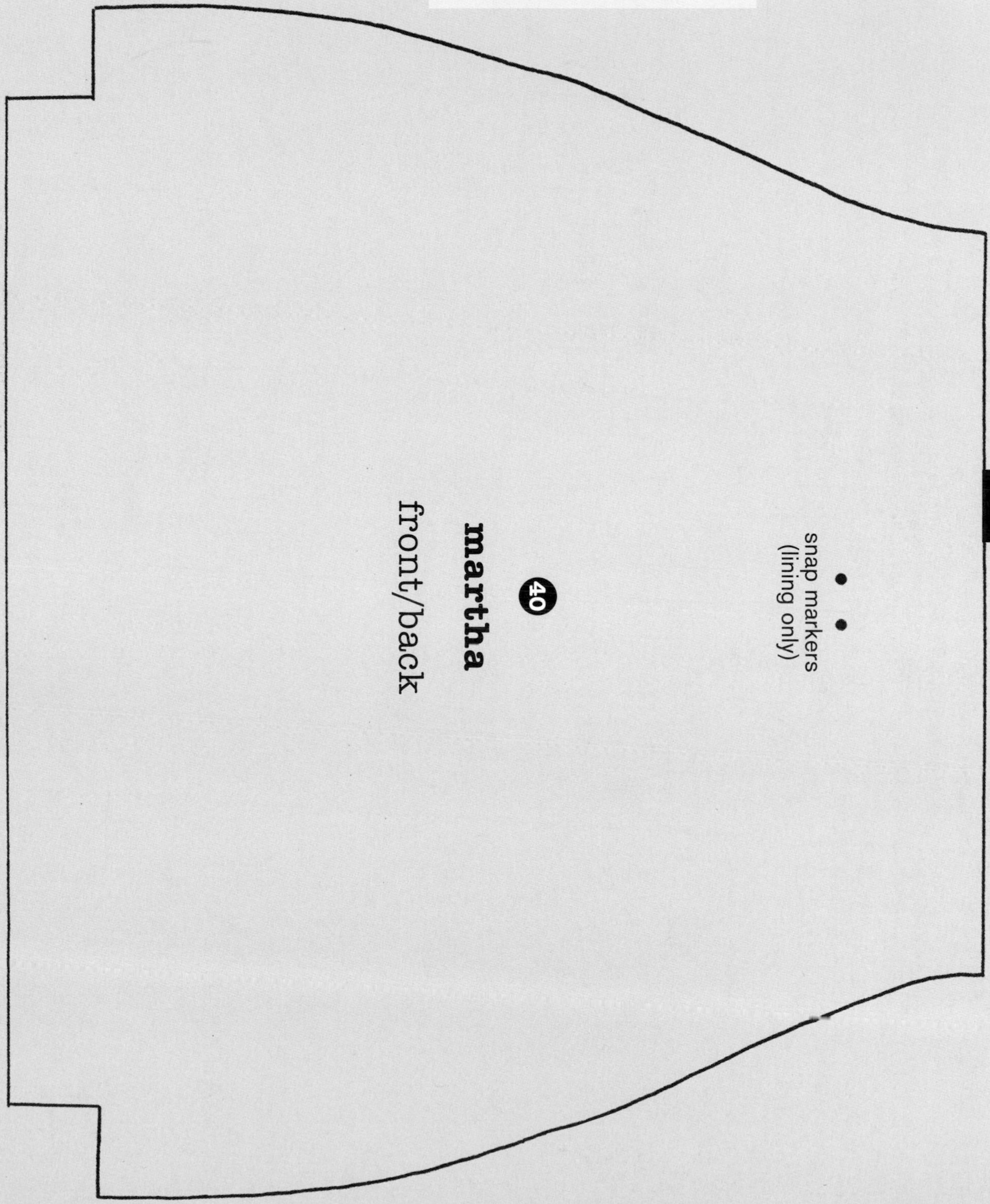

martha
front/back

④⓪

snap markers
(lining only)

151

pattern templates

making **vintage** bags

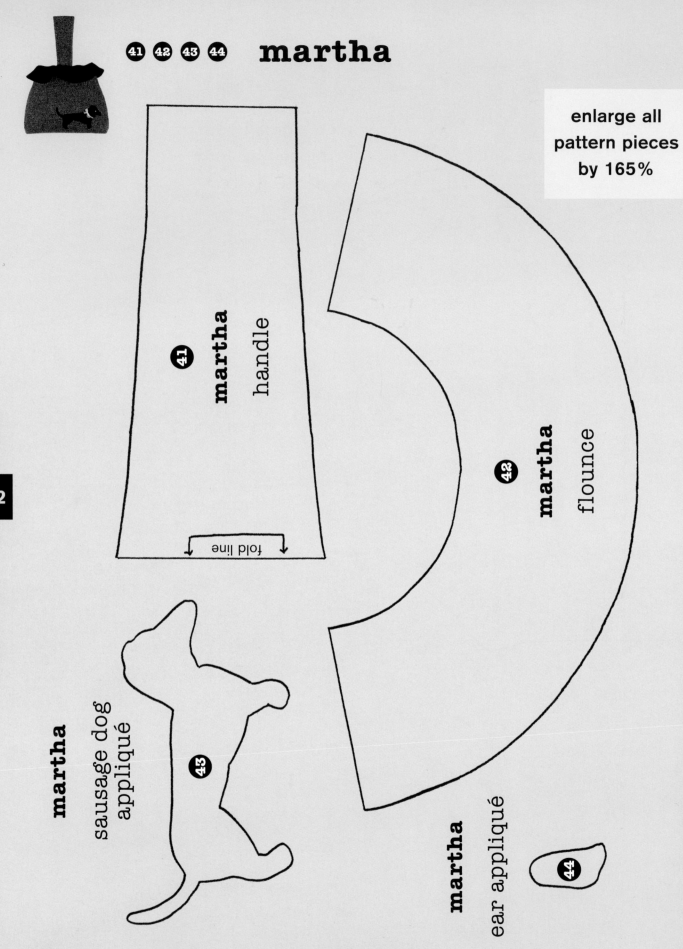

martha

㊶ ㊷ ㊸ ㊹

㊶ **martha**
handle

fold line

㊷ **martha**
flounce

martha
sausage dog appliqué

㊸

martha
ear appliqué

㊹

when photocopying, align dotted rule with top edge of glass

pattern templates

veronica ④⑤

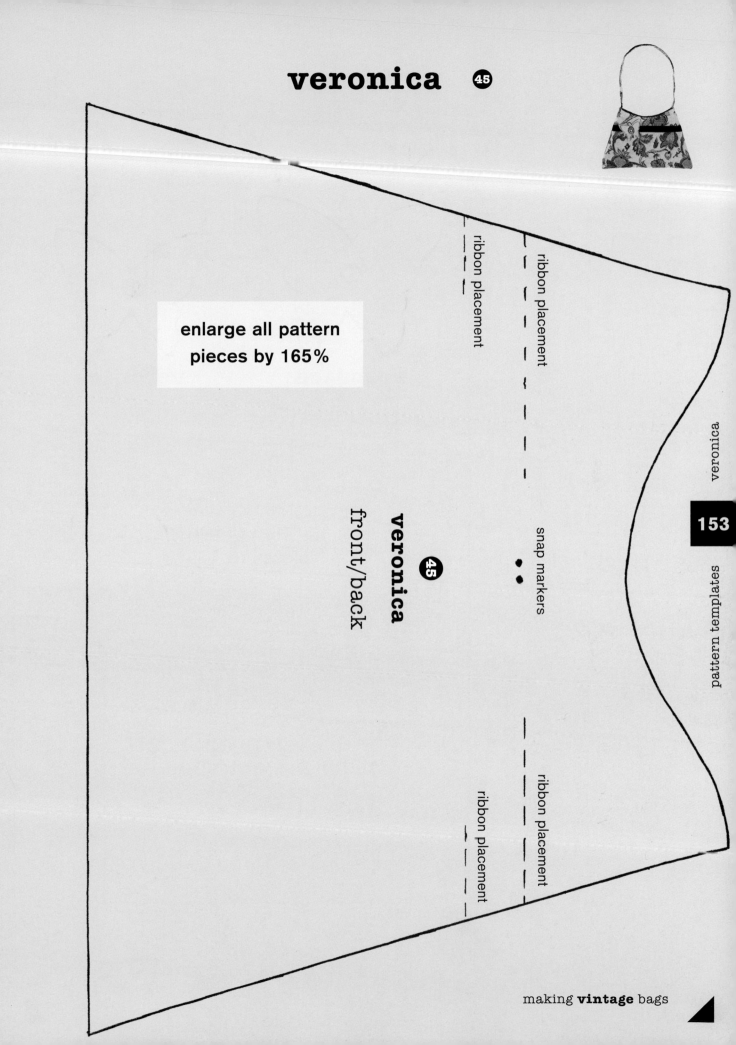

enlarge all pattern
pieces by 165%

ribbon placement

ribbon placement

veronica
front/back

④⑤

snap markers

ribbon placement

ribbon placement

46 47 48 # veronica

veronica

large butterfly

veronica

small butterfly

single fold handle

(finished width 1in (2.5cm))

46 veronica

↓ fold line ↓

enlarge all pattern
pieces by 165%

veronica

butterfly appliqué
for matching purse

when photocopying, align dotted rule with top edge of glass

grace ㊾

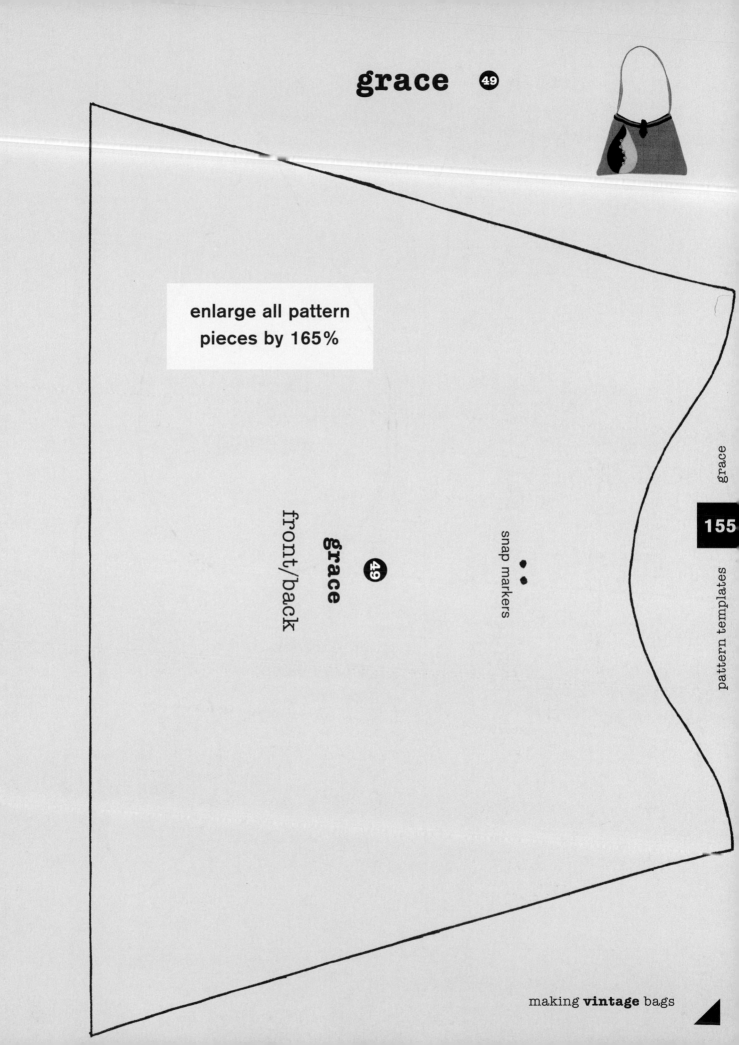

enlarge all pattern
pieces by 165%

grace
front/back

㊾

snap markers

50 51 52 grace

fold line

50

grace

double fold
handle

(finished width
¾in (18cm))

51

grace

main leaf
appliqué

enlarge all
pattern pieces
by 165%

52

grace

leaf overlay
appliqué

when photocopying, align dotted rule with top edge of glass

making **vintage** bags

patricia / rose ⑤③ ⑤⑤ ⑤⑧ ⑥⓪

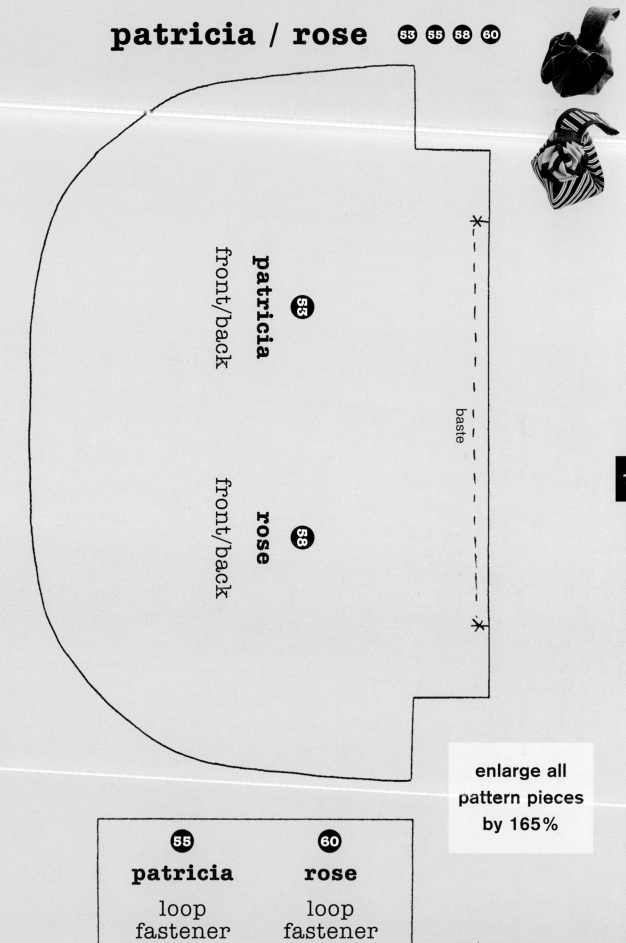

patricia
front/back ⑤③

rose
front/back ⑤⑧

baste

⑤⑤
patricia
loop
fastener

⑥⓪
rose
loop
fastener

enlarge all
pattern pieces
by 165%

54 56 57 59 **patricia / rose**

59

54 **patricia rose**

handle

handle

56 **patricia**

main bow piece

enlarge all pattern
pieces by 165%

when photocopying, align dotted rule with top edge of glass

57 **patricia**

bow centre

audrey ⑥① ⑥②

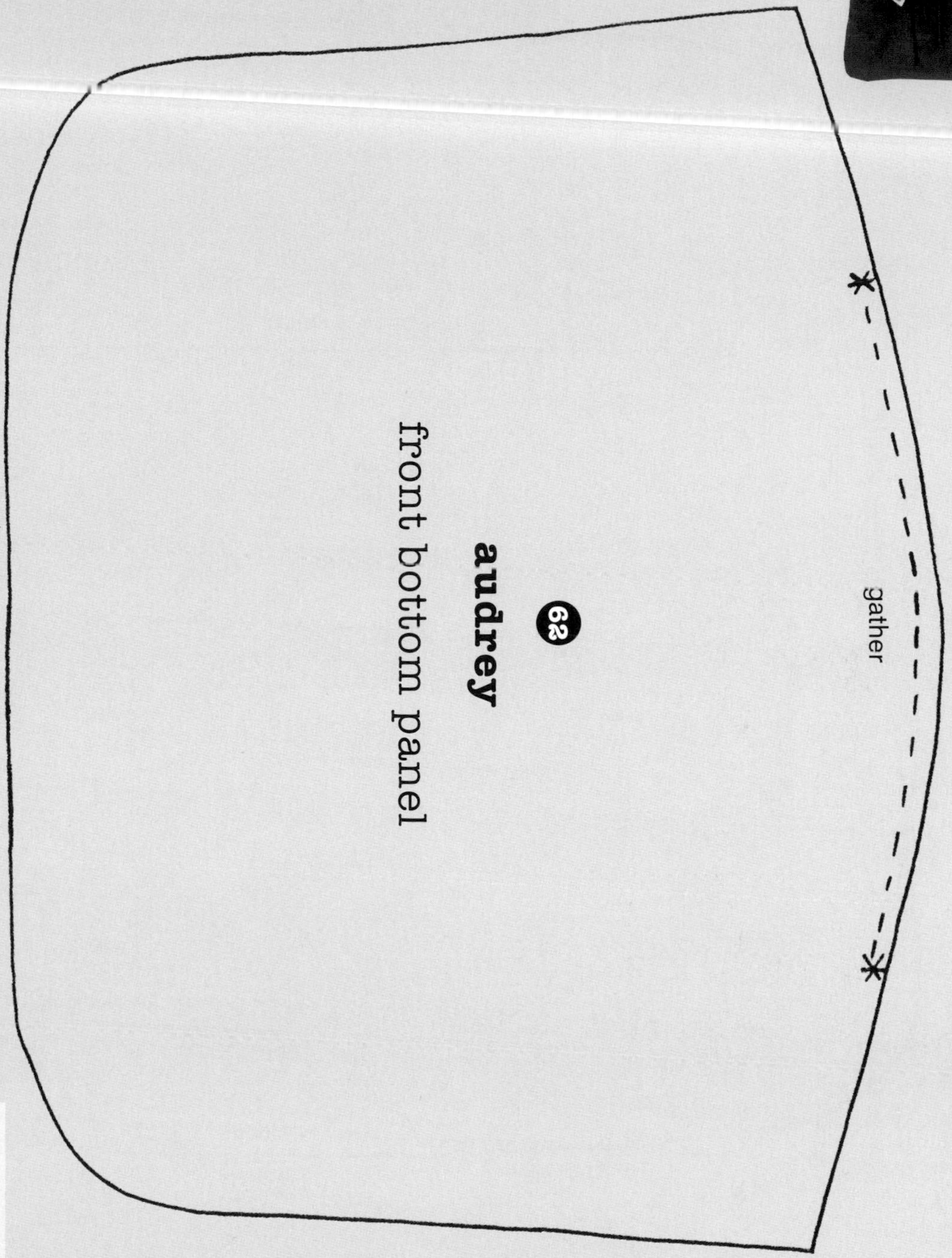

gather

audrey
front bottom panel

⑥②

enlarge all
pattern pieces
by 165%

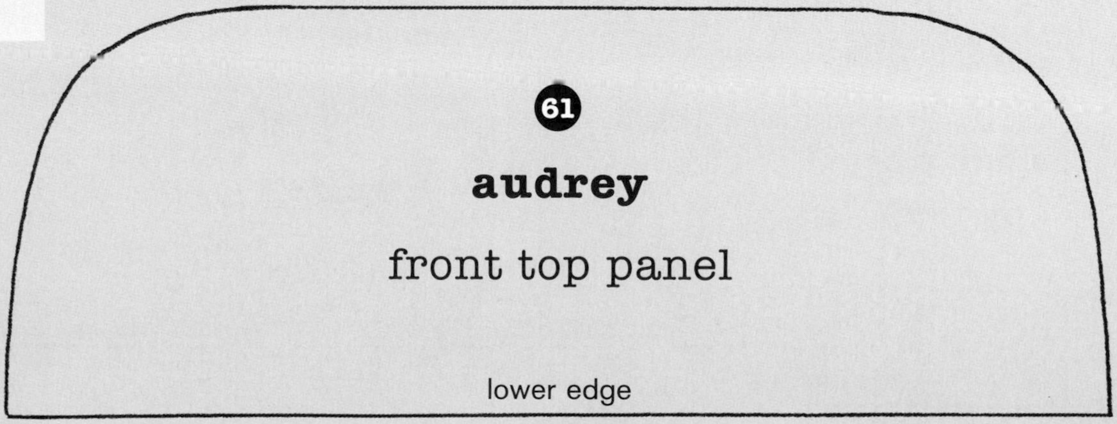

⑥①

audrey

front top panel

lower edge

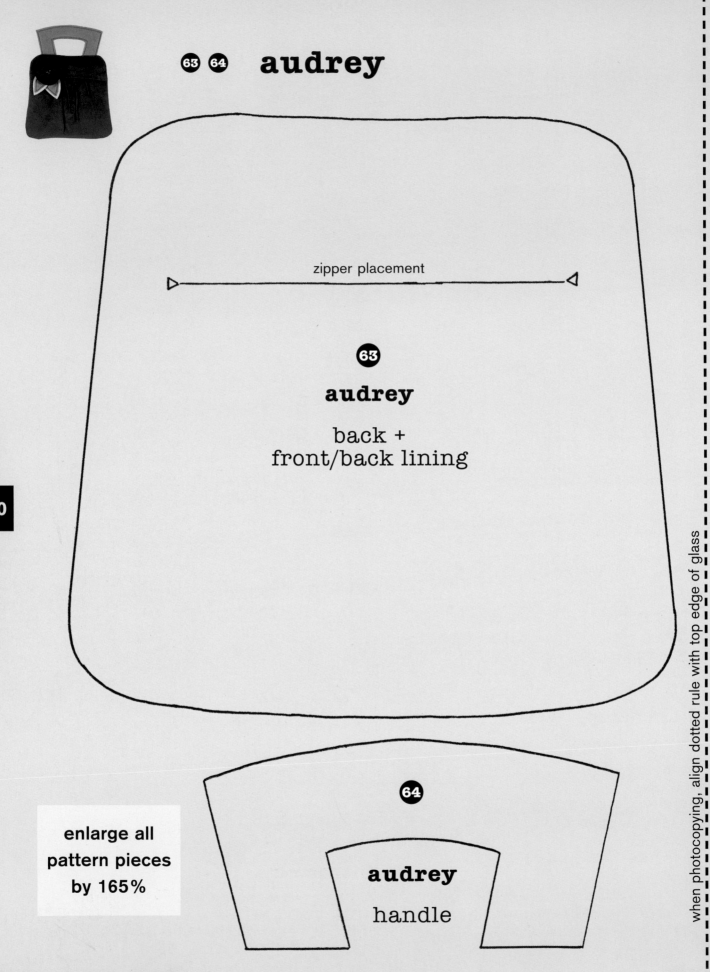

63 64 **audrey**

zipper placement

63

audrey

back +
front/back lining

64

audrey

handle

enlarge all
pattern pieces
by 165%

when photocopying, align dotted rule with top edge of glass

audrey ⑥⑤ ⑥⑥ ⑥⑦ ⑥⑧ ⑥⑨ ⑦⓪

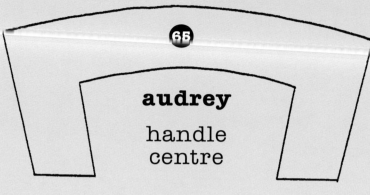

65

audrey

handle
centre

enlarge all pattern
pieces by 165%

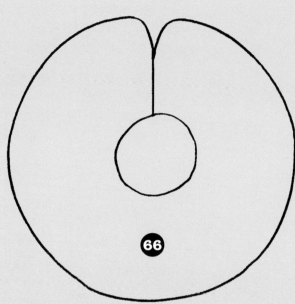

66

audrey

large petal

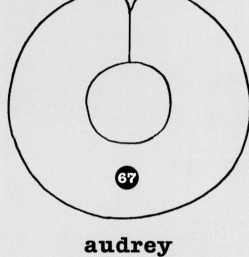

67

audrey

small petal

68

dart

audrey

large leaf

69

cart

audrey

medium leaf

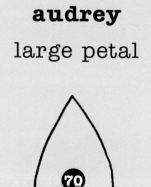

70

audrey

small leaf

71 72 **vivien**

72

vivien

snap markers

facing

lower edge

enlarge all pattern
pieces by 165%

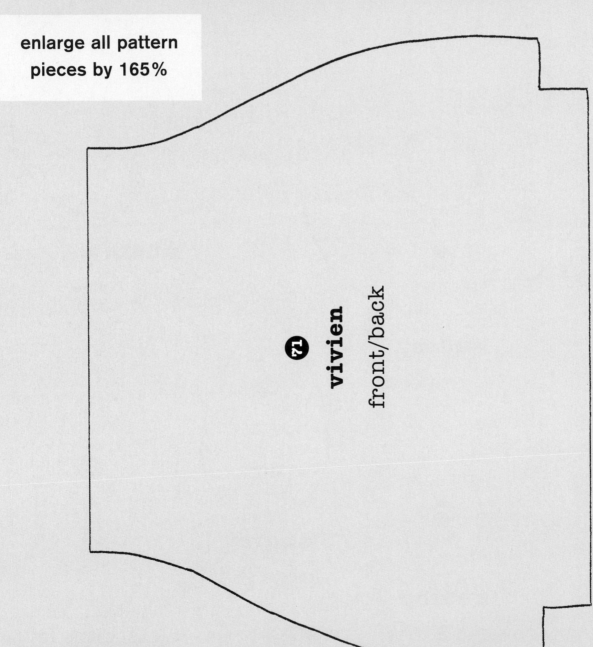

71 **vivien**
front/back

when photocopying, align dotted rule with top edge of glass

vivien ⓻⓭

enlarge all
pattern pieces
by 165%

vivien ⓻⓭

front/back
lining

upper edge

fold line

⓻⓭ **vivien**

handle

75 **76** **vivien**

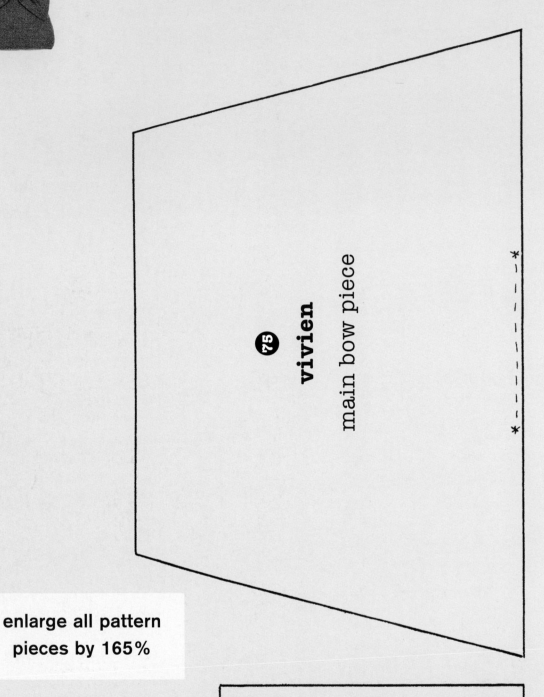

75

vivien

main bow piece

enlarge all pattern
pieces by 165%

76

vivien

bow centre

when photocopying, align dotted rule with top edge of glass

shirley ⑦ ⑦ ⑧ ⑧

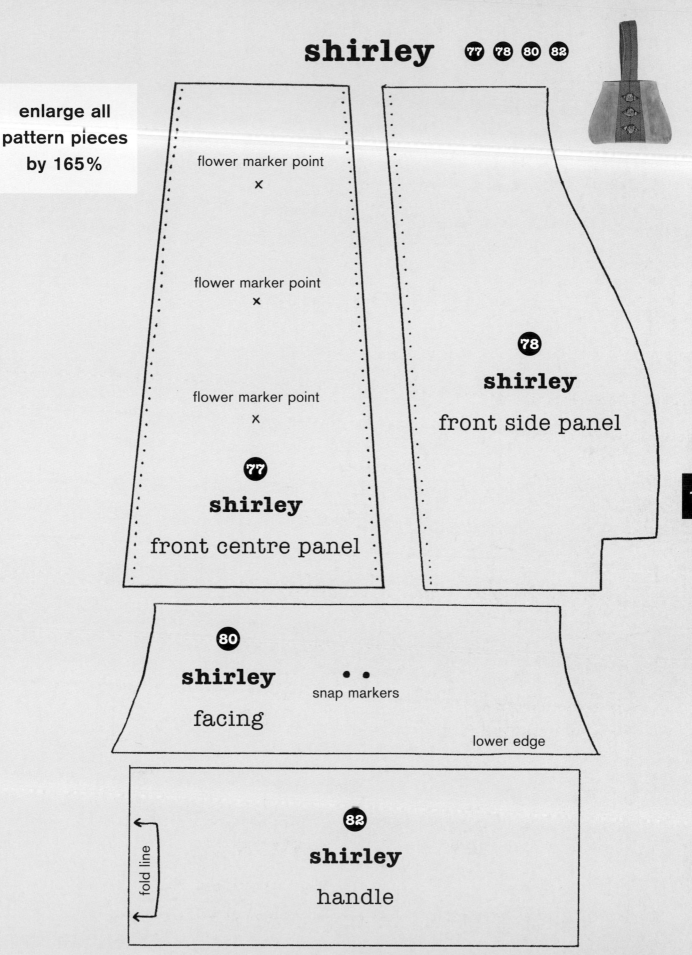

enlarge all
pattern pieces
by 165%

flower marker point
✗

flower marker point
✗

flower marker point
✗

78

shirley

front side panel

77

shirley

front centre panel

80

shirley

facing

snap markers

lower edge

82

shirley

handle

fold line

pattern templates

making **vintage** bags

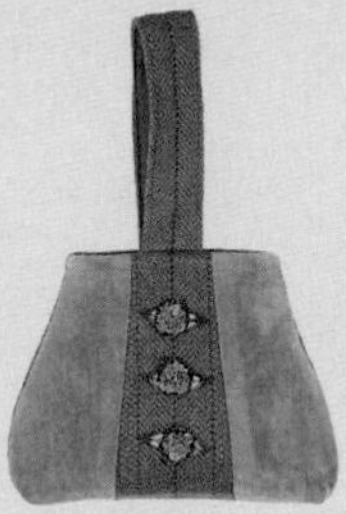

79 81 **shirley**

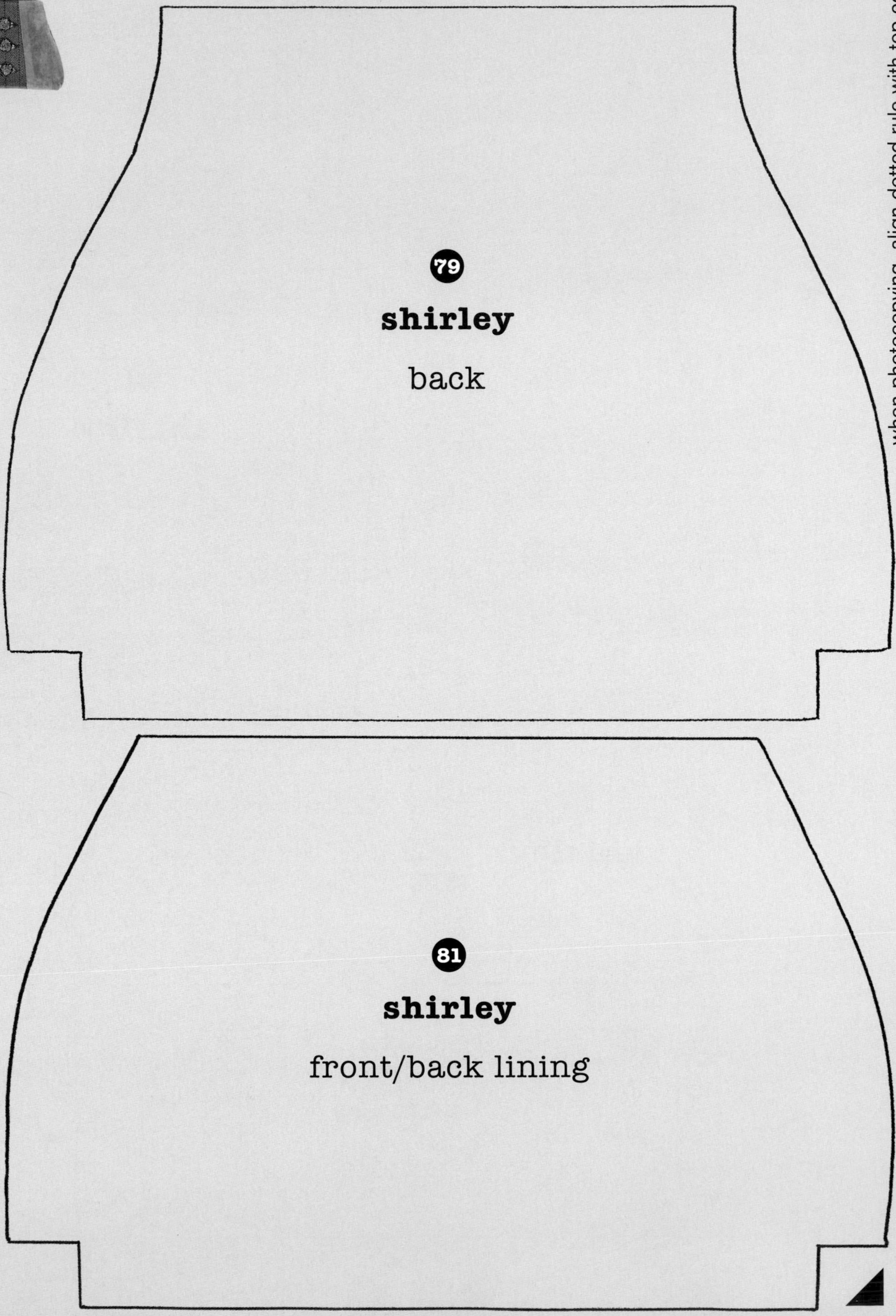

79

shirley

back

81

shirley

front/back lining

when photocopying, align dotted rule with top edge of glass

peggy / gloria ⑧③ ⑧⑧

join pattern piece to lower front/back at arrow

gloria
upper front/back

⑧⑧

peggy
upper front/back

⑧③

zip placement

join pattern piece to lower front/back at arrow

fold

enlarge all pattern pieces by 165%

join pattern piece to upper front/back at arrow

⑧③

peggy

lower front/back

⑧⑧

gloria

lower front/back

line

join pattern piece to upper front/back at arrow

84 **89** # peggy / gloria

enlarge all pattern pieces by 165%

84

peggy

front/back lining

89

gloria

front/back lining

fold line

when photocopying, align dotted rule with top edge of glass

*making **vintage** bags*

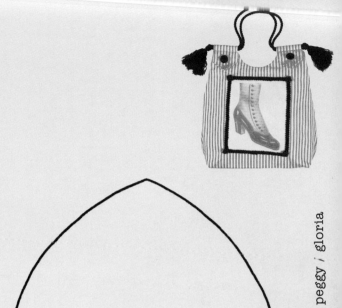

85

peggy

90

gloria

handle carrier
tabs

86

peggy

bow

87

peggy
bow centre

enlarge all pattern
pieces by 165%

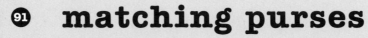
(91) matching purses

(91)

purse template

for 6in (15cm) zipper

**enlarge all pattern
pieces by 165%**

when photocopying, align dotted rule with top edge of glass

UK materials and suppliers

Panduro Hobby
Westway House
Transport Avenue
Brentford
Middlesex
TW8 9HF
Tel: 0208 8476161
www.panduro.co.uk

Suppliers of fabric, trims and craft materials, as well as handbag handles.

A. L. Maugham & Co Ltd.
5-7, Fazakerley Street (off Old Hall Street)
Liverpool
L3 9DN
Tel: 0151 236 1872

Suppliers mainly of soft leather, but also stock handbag fittings including magnetic snaps, and buckles. Mail order available.

MacCulloch & Wallis
25-26 Dering Street
London
W1S 1AT
Tel: 0207 6290311
www.macculloch-wallis.co.uk

Suppliers of fabrics, ribbons, trims, handbag handles, and magnetic snaps. Comprehensive mail order catalogue available.

Linton Tweeds
Shaddon Mills
Shaddongate
Carlisle
CA2 5TZ
www.lintontweeds.co.uk

Weavers of wonderful tweeds in wool and silk. Available at the Linton Fabric Centre and by mail order

suppliers

171

materials

US materials and suppliers

UMX – Universal Mercantile Exchange Inc.
21128 Commerce Point Drive
Walnut
CA 91789
USA
www.umei.com

Manufacturers of handbag-making supplies.
Huge range of handles, snaps, feet. Will also sell in
small quantities.

Renaissance Ribbons
P.O. Box 699
Oregon House
CA 95962
USA
www.renaissanceribbons.com

Wholesalers of ribbons, including vintage.
View selection online.

Fabric Direct
P.O. Box 7411
Newburgh
NY 12550
USA
www.fabricdirect.com

Suppliers of fabrics, including tweeds at very
reasonable prices. Purchase online.

Ultra Style Designs
813, Moffat Ct.
Castle Rock
CO 80108
USA
www.ultrastyledesigns.com

Suppliers of original Ultrasuede (fake suede fabric),
in a huge range of colours.

index

Page numbers in **bold** refer to illustrations

acknowledgements

Thank you to Mark, Mum and
Charlie for their support
throughout the project and to
Andy for the photograph of me!

GMC Publications would like to
thank the following people for
loaning props:

Virginia Brehaut, Stephen Haynes,
Gill Parris, Brigid Purcell, Gerrie Purcell.